$S: 2001$

Abby—Lost at Sea

To Nicholas,

Happy reading!

Aloha

Pamela Walls

SOUTH SEAS ADVENTURES

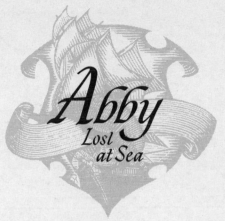

Abby
Lost
at Sea

PAMELA WALLS

TYNDALE HOUSE PUBLISHERS, INC.
WHEATON, ILLINOIS

Printed in the United States of America

09	08	07	06	05	04	03	02	01	00
10	9	8	7	6	5	4	3	2	1

TO THE ONE I LOVE
AND TO AMY, MANDY, AND TED, WHO KEPT ON BELIEVING.

*I am with you
and will watch over you wherever you go.*
GENESIS 28:15

Chapter One

OCTOBER 1847

Thirteen-year-old Abby Kendall brushed her long cinnamon curls off her shoulder, yawned, and returned to her writing task. This day in October had been unseasonably hot—*Indian summer* the residents of Pueblo de San Jose, California, called it—when the wind stilled and it seemed like the sky had forgotten to breathe.

The one-room schoolhouse was stuffy as a result. Although Abby didn't like most sports, she looked longingly out of the schoolhouse's one window and thought of the swimming hole at Coyote Creek. But all she could see was a distant row of alder trees, blue sky above, and heat waves shimmering on the glass.

The younger children, seated up front, were taking turns reading out loud while the teacher, Mrs. Jacinto, helped others at the blackboard. Abby glanced across the aisle at Luke Quiggley, her best friend. He caught her glance and rolled his eyes heavenward. His sun-streaked hair fell over one eye as he leaned toward her and whispered, "I'm 'board' as a fence. I'd rather go out and wake snakes."

She nodded with a grin, then turned her gaze to her slate work. But an unusual sound penetrated her heat-fogged brain.

Ker-thunk, ker-thunk.

Abby sat up straight. *What's that?* she wondered.

She looked toward the school's door. Someone, or something, was climbing the four wooden steps of the schoolhouse.

Ker-thunk, ker-thunk. It was unsettling.

As the door creaked open, Abby held her breath. A sense of doom, like a cold gust of wind, swept over her. Out of the corner of her eye, she saw Luke's head turn toward the door, too.

Ker-thunk. Ker-thunk.

Outlined against the October sky was a wide-chested sailor, who paused before he took a step inside. In a glance, Abby saw that he had only one good leg. His other was gone from the knee down, and in its place was a wooden peg.

Abby's eyes widened in awe. From his simple duck-cloth pants and cotton shirt, there was no doubt he was a sailor, but the peg leg gave him the air of a pirate.

Just then Mrs. Jacinto turned from the blackboard. "Who . . . who are you?" she asked in surprise.

McGuffey readers were forgotten as all heads turned to take in the stranger. The children instantly fell silent.

2

Ker-thunk, ker-thunk. The wooden leg sounded hollow on the floor as the stranger moved into the classroom. His dark eyebrows drew together. "I be lookin' fer one Abigail Kendall." His black eyes roamed the room.

Abby's hands grew clammy. She glanced at Luke, whose mouth hung open like a barn door, and swallowed. "I . . . uh . . . I'm Abby Kendall."

He started toward her . . . *ker-thunk, ker-thunk.* From somewhere behind her, Abby could hear Mrs. Jacinto say, "Here now, what's all this about?" But she couldn't take her eyes off the man limping toward her. He wore a silver earring that swayed each time he took a step. Reaching under his ratty vest, he pulled out a folded envelope.

By the time he drew to a stop in front of her, Mrs. Jacinto had hurried over to stand beside Abby. She laid a hand on Abby's shoulder, her fingers clutching.

The sailor cocked his head at the teacher. "I kin see you don't git many visitors here." When he laughed, Abby noted his blackened teeth.

Mrs. Jacinto pursed her lips and cleared her throat. "What can I do for you, sir?" Her voice sounded firm, but her fingers on Abby's shoulder trembled.

"The store owner told me Abigail was here. I got to git back to me ship, so I can't be running out to the country lookin' fer her pa."

Despite the sailor's somewhat ominous air,

Abby's curiosity flared. *Who is he, and why is he searching me out?*

"Have you come from the South Pacific, sir?" she asked, her heart thudding with anticipation.

"Aye, all the way from the Pacific Isles. And me cap'n has carried this with him." The sailor laid the envelope on her desk. Abby caught a strong smell of sweat and the faint odor of the briny sea.

With his callused hands he smoothed out the folded envelope on her desktop.

"This letter's from a Samuel Kendall," he said, one eyebrow raised as he glanced over Abby's head at the mesmerized faces of her classmates. "Me cap'n and him are mates, and I'm to deliver it to his kin."

"Uncle Samuel!" she said enthusiastically. *Oh, I hope he sent another story of the islands!* There was nothing Abby liked better than dreaming of adventure and travels with Luke—especially to faraway mysterious lands.

The sailor pinned her with a stare. "Carry it to yer pa fer me?"

Abby picked up the stained envelope and smiled. "I will. Thank you."

But the sailor had already turned toward the door, his peg leg thumping out an uneven beat. Then the door slammed behind him.

Everyone began talking at once. Mrs. Jacinto clapped her hands loudly. "Quiet!" She put one hand to her forehead. "Oh my, Abigail! I certainly hope your uncle won't be sending us any more surprise visitors."

Abby tucked the letter in her well-worn sketch-book and reluctantly set it aside. "I hope so, ma'am. I'm sorry for the interruption. But Uncle Samuel often sends word with sea captains coming our way." She looked over at Luke, who was trying to suppress a grin.

"Exactly where does your uncle live, Abigail?"

"In the Sandwich Islands, ma'am."

At that moment Sarah, Abby's eight-year-old sister raised her hand but didn't wait for Mrs. Jacinto to call on her. "Ma says that's where natives dance in the moonlight!"

"Sarah, that will be quite enough," Mrs. Jacinto said briskly. She gave some boys nearby a withering look that silenced them, but the rest of the class was too excited now to concentrate on seatwork.

"Boys and girls, it's near the end of the day. We'll dismiss early to the yard for a game of choose-up relays."

War whoops broke out as the children stam-peded through the door like a herd of buffalo.

"Abby! Abby!" Friends of all ages from the one-room school gathered around her, hoping to hear more about her uncle or the sailor with the wooden leg.

Sarah hurried over. "Were you scared, Abby?" she asked. "I was! He looked fierce, like one of those 'bucking-ears' we saw in Pa's book!"

Abby smiled and tossed her long hair off her shoulder. "That's buccaneers, Sissy."

Sarah's slate-blue eyes sparkled with excitement. "What happened to his other leg?"

"Probably got bitten off by a shark," Luke said authoritatively. His green eyes danced with the thrill of adventure. "Can't wait till we go traveling like him."

Abby's eyes took on a faraway look. "Oh, me too! Exotic islands and people of strange tongues. But," she vowed, coming back to the moment, "I'm bringing my toothbrush and powder. Did you see his teeth?"

"I bet he has bad breath," Sarah answered. "Nobody would kiss him, not even if he had a pirate treasure."

Luke laughed, but Abby shook her head at her sister. "Even sailors have feelings, Sarah. And God doesn't want us saying bad things about people."

"Oh, all right. His ma would probably kiss 'im— on the forehead." She kicked a dirt clod and ran off.

The sound of Mrs. Jacinto's wooden whistle called the children to order. As they grouped around her, she announced, "Jacob and Kyle will be team leaders today." A flurry of discussion followed. Never before had the ten-year-old boys been chosen as team captains for a relay race.

When Abby caught Luke's glance, she noticed that his smile had faded. Usually he was chosen as a team captain. And he always picked her first—even though she was the slowest runner at school. Everyone knew she'd inherited her ma's legs—some condition that caused her to run slow and tire easily. Now there wasn't a thing he could do for her.

Apprehension turned in Abby's stomach like sour milk, but she tried to joke about it. "Get ready for another show of the tortoise and the hare, with me in the losing role."

She gripped her cotton skirt to dry her clammy hands. One by one, the school children around her cleared out, each picked to join a team. Soon she was the oldest and tallest person left among a bunch of shrimps. To her horror, she was the *last* person picked. She took her spot on Jacob's team.

Luke looked over from Kyle's line. "Hey, they saved the best 'til last." She knew his smile was meant to encourage her, but she was too embarrassed to smile back. Two bright-red spots of humiliation bloomed on Abby's cheeks. Amid the hubbub of excited, jostling kids, only Abby noticed Luke slipping from the head of the line to take last place across from her.

Mrs. Jacinto raised her arm, dropped a white handkerchief, and the first runners took off. For the next few minutes, Luke's team surged ahead of Abby's, flying around the midway marker and returning first to pass the baton to the next in line. But halfway through, Abby's team gained the upper hand and was half a length ahead of Luke's.

The screams and shouts grew louder as the last

few runners waiting to take their turns drew to the head of the line. Abby's heart pounded. Her team was now a whole length ahead of Luke's. Even so, she didn't stand a chance. She had to run against Luke, the fastest boy at school! She would ruin it for her team, and everyone would hate her.

Abby drew to the head of the line, waiting for the baton as her teammate sprinted toward her. Luke stood across from her, waiting for his teammate, who still had not rounded the halfway marker. When Abby's teammate flew toward her, baton outstretched, she grabbed it and sprinted for all she was worth. She'd been given a good head start!

Abby clutched the baton in one sweaty hand and, with the other, grabbed her skirt to lift it out of the way. Her lungs ached and her eyes teared with the effort. She drove herself harder than she ever had before. She heard a groan go up just before she rounded the marker and started back toward the finish line. When she saw Luke bending over to pick up his dropped baton, she realized why his team had moaned. Now Luke leapt up and threw himself into the sprint.

Abby heard her teammates' cheers as she headed down the homestretch. She stood a chance! For the first time in her life, she might not lose a relay! She was halfway down the homestretch, and Luke was just rounding the marker. Nine-tenths of the way home, she could hear Luke's footsteps pounding behind her. The frenzied screams of her classmates told her the race was close, very close, though she didn't dare look over her shoulder.

Abby threw herself across the finish line, doubling over with heaving breaths. Never before had she thought there was a chance she could win against anyone, especially Luke! She straightened and felt classmates pounding her back. Sarah came over and gripped her hand. "You won!"

For a moment Abby basked in the joy—the reprieve from complete humiliation.

Then she saw Luke standing with his head down, one boot scuffing the dirt. His teammates quietly milled around. Mrs. Jacinto blew her whistle. "Good race!" she yelled. "Now everyone collect your books. Class dismissed."

Luke looked up then, his eyes grazing Abby's happy face. They exchanged smiles, and just before heading into the classroom, he winked at her. That's when Abby knew. He had dropped the baton on purpose to give her more time!

She followed his tall form as they headed into the classroom. Gathering her sketchbook and slate into the leather carrying strap, she swallowed the emotion that was rising like a lump in her throat.

Oh Luke, she thought, tightening her book strap, *you're the best friend I've ever had.*

Abby never suspected that the letter swinging in her sketchbook was about to change all that.

Chapter Two

"Did you ever hear about the tortoise who swallowed some gun powder?" Luke asked Abby, Sarah, and Jacob on the walk home from school.

Sarah, in a red calico dress and white pinafore, looked up eagerly at Luke. "No, what happened?"

"Well, he shot right past the hare, won the race, and was the guest of honor at the victory dinner." Luke paused to glance at Abby. "Where they served grilled tortoise steaks."

Sarah and Jacob giggled. Abby cocked an eyebrow. "Even so, I'm sure that turtle appreciated winning for once in her life. And as for the dinner— that rabbit deserved it."

Sarah looked confused, then shrugged and skipped ahead of them on the dirt road.

Luke glanced over at Abby. "Are you gonna read that letter?"

She gripped the leather strap that held her slate and sketchbook. "I'm dying to, but this one is addressed to Pa."

"Nettles and rats," Luke said, "I guess I'll have to wait till tomorrow to hear your uncle's news." Turning to Jacob, he asked, "Are the fish still biting at Coyote Creek?"

Abby soon lost interest in their conversation. When she spotted a flash of blue on a nearby birch tree, she quickly unbuckled her book strap, flipped open her tattered sketchbook, and grabbed the pencil from her pinafore pocket. Her eyes narrowed as she focused on the bluejay before her, capturing its likeness in quick strokes. The jay cocked its head sideways as if to say, "Did you get my best profile?"

By now Sarah stood waiting far ahead of the others. She looked back and frowned, her white-blonde hair coming loose from its single braid, her eyes snapping with irritation. "Abby, come on!" she hollered from the bend in the road that led to their three-room cabin. "Ma's probably got hot cookies waiting!"

Abby returned to her drawing, too busy to mind Sarah. But a sudden whack on her back jolted the pencil, sending a crooked line across the paper. "Luke!" she growled, turning her wide-set eyes on him. The bluejay cawed loudly and flew off, a brilliant splash of larkspur against the now gray sky.

Luke grinned down at her, the dimple in his left cheek puckering. Green eyes sparkled with mischief. "Aw, Abby, why do you need to draw it when we've got millions of them—everywhere?" he said, glancing around the countryside. His finger tweaked her slightly upturned nose.

Abby's mouth drew into a straight line. "Haven't you ever heard of art . . . culture . . . civilized enjoyment?"

"Who wants to sit around drawing," he asked, "or writing poems when there's a whole world out there waiting to be explored?" He was forever growing impatient with her stopping to draw or write down a poem. Once he had accused her of carrying quotes in her memory like most people carried peppermints in their pockets.

"For your information, a lot of people love art and pay good money for books of it." Abby closed her sketchbook, tightened the strap, and jammed the pencil behind her ear. She sighed as she started down the road. "How do you think Mr. Joseph Banks, the botanist who traveled with Captain Cook on his sailing adventures, made all his money?"

"Art?" Luke questioned, one nut-brown eyebrow arched.

Abby nodded. "He's famous for recording all the beautiful flora and fauna in the South Pacific."

Luke frowned. "What do floors and fawns have to do with art?"

Abby shook her head. "Flora and fauna—it means the plant and animal life of all the islands he visited! Luke, you frustrate the freckles off me!"

He ignored her comment. "So, he made money off his traveling adventures? That's one smart dandy," Luke said as he stuck a blade of grass between his lips. He brushed his straight hair off his forehead. "Keep it up, then, Ab. Maybe someday you can make us some money. That'll help when we set off on adventures."

Abby grinned in spite of herself. She and Luke had been dreaming of traveling since they'd first met three years ago when he'd come west from Pennsylvania alone. For the past three harvests Luke had worked alongside Pa and had become a welcome addition to their family—sort of the son Pa had never had—even though he lived with his rich aunt, D. G.

"Maybe we'll follow in Mr. Banks's footsteps," Luke continued, looking up at the tree limbs moving in a gust of wind. "We could make our first stop your uncle's ranch in the Sandwich Islands."

Abby bit her lip. They had pored over every letter Uncle Samuel had written and memorized the map of the islands he'd drawn. "Maybe. I can't wait to read his latest letter."

Luke did a handstand and walked forward on his palms, legs straight in the air. "Let me know what's new," he said, flipping to a standing position. "See you later." He waved and took the left fork in the road.

For a minute Abby watched his back. Then she called out, "Can the hare join the tortoise for a victory supper tonight?"

Luke turned. "Got too many chores. Maybe

14

mañana," he said, using the Spanish word for
tomorrow. The Mexicans still ruled California, and
the newly arriving Americans had adopted some of
their Spanish words.

Abby waved at him. "It's probably for the best.
We're having rabbit stew." Luke's mouth dropped
open. Then he shook his head with a smile and
headed down the lane that led to his aunt's
mansion.

Abby looked up. Gray clouds had already moved
in to cover the pine-green Santa Cruz Mountains
off in the distance, and the wind carried the scent of
rain.

Turning toward home, she saw pint-sized Sarah
standing in a wide-legged stance with her hands on
her hips. "You're *sooo* slow," Sarah accused before
she raced ahead, reaching their small cabin at the
end of the lane first.

"Not today!" Abby yelled back, remembering her
sweet victory. She watched her nimble sister climb
the old apricot tree beside the cottage.

At their yard Abby balanced her schoolbooks on
the fence post, then took hold of the water pump
handle. The metal was cold to the touch. After three
pumps, the silver liquid gushed out in a stream that
hit the rocks below. Droplets spattered her dusty
high-button shoes as she leaned over, took a long
drink, and then cooled her flushed face.

She dried her cheeks on the sleeve of her cream
cotton blouse. "Come on," she called over her

shoulder as she picked up her books. But Sarah paid her no mind as she swung upside down from the limb, skirt over her face, pantaloons bared to the world. Abby climbed the porch steps and opened the cottage door. "Ma!" she called. "We got a letter from Uncle Samuel today!"

Charlotte Kendall looked up from her work of cutting potatoes at the kitchen table. "Really?" she asked, her soft brown eyes full of wonder. "Who delivered it?"

Just then Sarah hurtled through the front door. "A pirate, Ma! He was big and ugly with a wooden leg, and he smelled something fierce, too."

Ma's eyes reflected surprise, but Abby agreed with Sarah's description. "It's true, Ma." She laid her books on the table and retrieved the letter, handing it over.

Her mother wiped her hands on her apron and carefully slit open the envelope with her paring knife. She silently scanned the letter, ignoring Sarah's pleas that she read it aloud.

Then Abby watched in surprise as her mother untied her apron and patted her bun neatly. Picking up the letter, Ma calmly put it back in the envelope. "Abby, see to the potatoes and the sweeping. I'm going to find your father."

Abby's eyes widened. Her mother never went looking for their father two hours before he was due home. Abby watched her mother disappear out the door, then went in search of the broom.

If there was one thing Abby hated in life, it was sweeping. But at the moment, she didn't feel like complaining. She could hear Sarah whining that Ma had left without giving her a snack to eat, but Abby didn't respond. Something else was speaking louder. It was that little voice of warning that had begun when she heard the first *ker-thunk* on the schoolhouse steps.

Now that feeling of premonition was stronger than ever. What was in the letter that would cause Ma to go find Pa? Abby had a feeling she wasn't going to like the answer.

Chapter Three

Abby swept all three rooms of their cabin and added potatoes to the rabbit stewing in the iron pot, which hung over the fire. Then she and Sarah went for a walk to while away the time until Ma returned.

When they got back, Sarah climbed her tree beside the cottage while Abby went inside. She stopped short when she saw both her parents seated at the kitchen table. Thomas Kendall, her pa, was home earlier than usual. His big hand was wrapped around a mug of coffee as it rested on the red-checkered tablecloth. Abby noticed a streak of dirt on Pa's cheek and the dark-blonde hair, as unruly as her own, that curled over his shirt collar.

For a few seconds no one spoke. Abby heard the ticking of the wind-up regulator clock on the wall and the soft bubbling of potatoes in the pot. Her mother looked up from her spot at the table.

"Abby, sit down," she said. "We have something to tell you."

Her stomach tightened at the serious tone in her mother's voice. *Did someone die?*

Pa brushed the bread crumbs off the tablecloth with his massive hands. "Abigail, you know we received a letter from your Uncle Samuel today. In fact, I hear a pretty colorful character delivered it. Well, he brought important news. My brother is ailing bad. It's a fever that comes and goes and leaves him weak. I guess he's been suffering for months now. He's asked us to come help him with the ranch."

Abby's heart quickened with hope. It would be wonderful to see the Sandwich Islands, the mysterious people, and the fragrant flowers Uncle Samuel had written about!

Abby caught her mother's loving gaze. "Honey, your father and I have to help out family. We've decided to leave immediately. Uncle Samuel needs us, and you know there isn't much here to tie us down."

Abby knew her mother meant they didn't own land in Pueblo de San Jose. But when she suddenly thought of Luke, her heart raced. "Ma, what about Pa's job on Mr. Morgan's ranch, and all our friends?" She and Luke had dreamed of traveling, but not this week! "And what about Luke? Can we bring him with us? I mean, he'd be lost without our family!" *And he's my best friend!*

"Princess," her father said, using the nickname he usually reserved for tender moments, "I'm planning on talking with Luke's aunt, but don't set a store on her answer."

"Oh, Pa, we've got to bring him with us!" Abby cried. Instinctively her hand went to her throat and the cross hanging there. Formed of thin gold filigree, the cross hung on a delicate chain. It had been a birthday gift from Luke a year ago.

Her father got up from the table and came over to her. His dusty boots were big—everything about him was big. As Abby looked up into his face, she saw a reflection of her own twilight-blue eyes. Then she saw the tense line of Pa's mouth relax. "Princess, you know I want Luke along as much as you do, but we'll have to abide by his aunt's decision."

Abby's eyes blazed. "Pa, she won't do what's best for him! She's never been kind, not even when he first got here. That woman's dark, Pa. Her heart's filled with poison!"

"Abigail, it's best not to judge what you don't know. Your pa will do all he can," her mother said firmly. Ma's mink-brown eyes softened as she brushed a stray hair from Abby's face.

Abby's tortured look wove back and forth between her parents. They were united in the decision! But the thought of leaving her home and best friend, even if only for a few months, made her mad. "How long will we be gone?" she demanded.

When her parents looked at one another gravely, she knew what their silence meant. "You can't mean

21

we're going to live there forever!" She made a strangled noise and jumped up from the chair. "I won't!"

Abby ran out of the house, letting the door slam behind her, and raced down the steps and across the yard. When she turned her ankle on a rock, she winced in pain but refused to slow down.

Sarah stopped swinging from the tree limb and dropped to the ground as she watched Abby limp by, tears tracking down her cheeks.

"What's wrong?" she asked Abby's retreating back.

Too mad to stop, Abby shouted her outrage over her shoulder. "Ma and Pa want to move to Uncle Samuel's—all the way to the Sandwich Islands!"

"You mean where the natives dance in the moonlight?" Sarah sounded awestruck. As Abby glanced back over her shoulder, she could see Sarah's little blonde eyebrows arched in amazement.

"That's right," Abby said, grateful that her sister grasped the horror of the situation.

"Ma!" Sarah yelled. "Ma!"

Ma opened the front door and stepped onto the narrow porch, concern etched across her face. Abby limped down the dirt road, but she could still hear Sarah's voice.

"Ma, is it true? Are we going to Uncle Samuel's to have a real adventure?" Stunned, Abby's mouth dropped open. *Traitor! Can't she see it means leaving all our friends behind?* she thought.

Just then Abby heard her father's boots on the

porch boards. "That's right, Little Britches," he answered gaily. "We're going to take a schooner and sail across the wide Pacific Ocean. It's a chance to own some land and start a new life."

Abby sped up her pace, even though her ankle now throbbed. *I don't want a new life! Not without Luke! And you shouldn't either!*

She was almost out of earshot, yet she could feel her mother's eyes boring into her back—all the way across the orchard of mustard seed and apricot trees. But she would not turn around and acknowledge those eyes.

Mother could have stopped this. Why didn't she? Doesn't she know it will break Luke's heart if we leave him behind?

A crow landed in a nearby alder tree. *Caw! Caw! Caw!* The mournful cry mirrored her own heart.

The wind carried the earthy scent of creek water across her path. Autumn leaves swirled free of their golden-brown piles and scuttled crablike across the road. Even if it wasn't almost time for the winter sun to set, the approaching clouds would darken the landscape soon.

Oh! Why did I ever bring that letter home? she wondered. The day had dawned just like any other, but it had brought the worst news of her life.

Her tea-colored hair swirled across her face, blocking her view. *That's just how things are, too. Like I can't see the future anymore.*

She had always thought her family would stay in

Pueblo de San Jose until she and Luke were grown enough to go off on their own. An hour ago she had longed for adventure—but never without Luke!

How could she tell him they were leaving? She remembered his wink at her this afternoon and tears flooded her eyes. She knew how much he counted them as his own family. More than anyone else, she knew what it'd done to him to be abandoned once before.

Off in the distance, the ominous rumble of thunder boomed across the Santa Clara Valley. But Abby didn't need to hear it to know she was walking straight into a storm.

Chapter Four

Abby walked a long time in the darkening twilight. Although her tears had long since dried, a heavy sadness had settled over her.

She had not consciously planned to go to Luke's home, but suddenly there she was at the gate that led up to the whitewashed mansion.

Sparks, the collie, whined a greeting and put his muzzle in her hand. She rubbed his head. "Where's Luke, boy?" she asked. The dog seemed to sense her emotion and whined again, prancing back and forth beside her.

"Find Luke," Abby commanded, and the collie bounded off toward the barn. Abby followed quickly; she didn't want to be seen by Luke's Aunt Dagmar.

She passed the open barn door and the warm scent of cows filled her nose. The barn was quiet except for the sound of hay being tossed. In the dim lantern light, Abby could see Luke standing near a huge pile of straw with a pitchfork in hand.

He wiped his forehead with the back of his hand

and dug into the pile. Again, she was struck by how much he had grown in the last few months. Years of hard work on the farm had made him muscular and athletic. She knew he loved it, as if his body needed to move. She suspected the work also reminded him of happier days in Pennsylvania before his ma and pa had died of cholera, before he'd been forced to come live with his aunt.

Abby had no idea when she reached out to the lonely stranger at school that he would turn out to be her best and most loyal friend. He didn't care that she had inherited a leg weakness that doctors said would never get better. "Abby, it just slows you down a bit. But you're a lot quicker," he had said, tapping her forehead, "up here than most."

She remembered the first day she'd asked him home for cookies after school. He had jumped at the offer of friendship as if he were starved for warmth.

"Aunt Dagmar runs her home with an iron hand in a silk glove," he'd told her. She'd heard about Dagmar Gronen before Luke arrived and knew she was considered a hard businesswoman. There would never be love to spare at the Gronen mansion, but Abby's family had plenty to share. So began a companionship that had sunk deep roots into both of them.

Now Sparks bounded over to Luke, as if he were proud of the present he'd brought his master. Luke paused in his work and saw Abby outlined against the doorway.

"Abby, what brings you here this late?" Luke asked.

She moved toward him but did not respond. There was a lump in her throat now that she saw him.

Luke dropped the pitchfork and strode over to her. "What's wrong?" Then, seeing the look on her face, he grabbed her arm. "Tell me." His voice was brusque.

"My uncle's sick. . . . He's asked us to move to the Sandwich Islands to help out with his ranch."

Luke dropped her arm and turned away. "And your parents are going to move?" He finished her sentence.

"Yes, but they want you to come, too. Pa is going to talk to your aunt and ask her." Abby spoke rapidly, trying to take away the pain she'd inflicted on him.

"She'll never let me go," he said flatly. "Her biggest enjoyment is controlling me. She can't do that if I'm not here."

"Oh, Luke . . ." Abby sighed. She needed to talk it all out with her best friend, but everything she said hurt him terribly. "What are we going to do?" she asked as she sank to her knees in the pile of straw. Tears brimmed on her spiky brown eyelashes.

Luke kicked the hay and stalked away in silence. He walked over to old Bessie and slapped the cow's rump in irritation. The roan lowed in protest and swung her head around to look at him with liquid eyes while he leaned his head against the Guernsey's warm side.

His silence spoke volumes, she realized. He was struggling to regain control.

But if Luke had been given to feeling sorry for himself, it would have been a finely developed trait in him by now. She watched him in the dim light. His head finally came up and his shoulders straightened. He walked over and kneeled in the hay next to her.

"One thing I know," he said. "You have to make your own way in life. People are always gonna let you down . . . or leave you."

Abby looked into his handsome face, the straight nose and strong chin, the blazing green eyes that stared unflinchingly into hers. "Yes," she said slowly, "people do, but God . . . doesn't." She wondered if she truly believed that herself. For years she had followed her parents to church, had sung the hymns, and had memorized Bible verses. But her life had never been tested—not really until this moment. Now, doubts were piling up like drifts of snow in a winter storm. *How could God let this happen?*

Luke picked up the little cross on her neck and smiled. "I knew my mother's cross would wear well on you. It needed someone who has the kind of faith she had, and that sure ain't me."

Abby bit her lower lip. *It might not be me either, Luke.*

He walked away, shaking his head. "Come on,"

he said, "I'll take you home. I know it's too long a
walk for you both ways."

Grabbing the bridle from the tack room, he fit it
cleanly over Lightning's head. In a fluid motion he
leapt up onto the bay's back and brought her
around to stand next to a hay bale.

Abby climbed up on the hay bale and mounted
behind him. Just then thunder boomed overhead,
like giants smashing boulders above them. "What
about your aunt? You'll be late for supper," she said.

"Right now, I don't care about that." He leaned
over to blow out the lantern hanging by the door.
His voice was tight with restrained anger.

The gray shadow of the open barn door had been
replaced by inky blackness. They headed out into it.

"Hold on tight, Abby. I'm in a mood to gallop."
He spurred the horse down the dark lane, and Abby
clung hard to Luke's waist as they tore down the
road, her hair bouncing wildly behind her. Her
curls were going to be an impossible snarl tonight.
Just like the rest of her life.

Then the clouds burst open, and cold rain slanted
across their faces.

Luke returned twenty minutes later, soaked to the
bone and shivering with cold. He lit the barn

lantern and began wiping down Lightning with burlap sacks. The mare snorted and stamped her foot, her sides still warm from galloping.

Suddenly a shadow crossed the lantern light. Before he even turned around, he sensed her presence.

"You're late." Luke flinched at the sound of Dagmar Gronen's voice. She stood in her black silks, holding a wet black parasol above her head. Her steel-gray hair was swept into a bun at the nape of her neck, but none of this softened her demeanor.

Luke had come to notice the slight curl of her upper lip when she caught him doing something for which she could punish him. He knew that she would enjoy the next few moments, for he had given her the perfect opportunity. He was late for supper. In her palace, one did not break with the expected dinnertime—or any of the many rules—and get away with it.

"I apologize for being late, Aunt Dagmar. It's my fault." He had learned that admitting his mistake right away took some of the starch out of her anger.

"You are wet! Don't you dare enter my home dripping. You will take your clothes off here and dry off with the burlap."

"But Aunt, I've got nothing else to put on!" Shock made him break with his own rule of quiet acceptance. He thought of Maria the cook and Corbin the butler. He'd have to wear burlap sacks into the house!

"You should have thought of that before you decided to delay our scheduled supper." Dagmar brushed a strand of wiry hair from her forehead and sniffed. "Corbin can bring something out for you to wear, but there will be no visiting friends tomorrow."

Luke hung his head and balled his fists. When he looked up, his neck cords stood out and his eyes smoldered, but he forced his voice to remain flat. "Whatever you say, Aunt."

Dagmar's nose lifted. Luke watched her scrutinize him, and he recognized the joy flooding her cold eyes. She held power over him as his legal guardian. "Good," she said. She clutched her skirt and walked toward the door.

As she lifted the parasol higher over her head, she looked back. "You will come to see, Luke, that I am right. Abide by my rules, and you will someday inherit my wealth. And that could certainly change the life of one penniless orphan boy." She strode out into the rain, soon blending into the blackness.

Luke's fists clenched and unclenched while his mind burned. "I don't want your ever-loving money!" he whispered fiercely. "You can keep it. Take it to the grave, for all I care."

Chapter Five

Three days later, Abby was setting the table when she realized she was daydreaming again. Pictures of distant islands and turquoise seas flitted across her mind. She tried to picture the strange-looking trees, like upside-down broomsticks, which her uncle had once described. In her imagination she saw these palm trees swaying over white sand and hidden treasure chests. For a fleeting minute she felt excited and then . . . like a traitor! *How can I look forward to going unless Luke is coming, too?*

When the front door opened, Abby looked up from setting the dinner table, her face frozen in a half-smile of hope. Pa walked in, but his usual grin was missing.

"Abby, I tried my best with Luke's aunt." He sighed softly and glanced away.

Abby's stomach lurched. "What, Pa?"

His eyes brimmed with compassion. "I couldn't sway her, Princess. I'm sorry."

The plate slipped from Abby's hand and clattered onto the wooden tabletop. "No, Pa! Luke has to come! Don't you see, we have to go around his aunt. You can't do this!"

"Abby." He came toward her and drew her against his chest, smoothing the back of her head. Abby relaxed against him. His shirt smelled like warm raisins. She trusted him; anytime she'd had a problem, Pa had always done his best to help her. He'd find a way now.

He brushed a curl off her forehead and clasped her face between his hands. "We have to do this the right way. She's his legal guardian. It might not be the best thing in our eyes, but God's allowed it for some reason, Princess."

Abby stiffened and pulled away. "Maybe God doesn't have anything to do with it! Maybe she's just mean and controlling like Luke says. It's not fair!"

"No, it doesn't seem fair. I love that boy like my own son. But I believe with all my heart that God loves him more, Abby." He shook his head quietly in a gesture of surrender, then dragged an unsealed envelope from his shirt pocket. When he laid it on the table, Abby saw four tickets sticking from the opened back—four passages to a distant land. Luke would stay behind.

Abby burst into tears.

Her father quietly pulled her into his arms and let her cry.

Two days later, Abby wearily wrapped a china teacup in an old dishtowel. Her family's life in California had been reduced to the three large trunks they were allowed aboard ship. She glanced through the one opened before her: Here was the wire corn popper they held over the fireplace in winter and outdoor campfires in summer; old towels; the enamel coffeepot that simmered each morning; Pa's leather gloves and hand tools, greased, then wrapped as well.

Clothing had easily fit into one trunk, since she and Sarah only owned three outfits apiece, plus two nightdresses and undergarments. Both would wear their warmest dresses, plus cloaks, and take one dress each in a satchel to wear later on the ship. Bedding and two quilts that she and her mother had sewn rested on top of their meager store of clothing. Sarah's rag doll would be carried in eager arms. Abby's sketchbook and Ma's family Bible would be lovingly carried in the carpetbag along with hairbrushes, toothbrushes, and a tin of home-baked molasses and oatmeal cookies. Pa had said ship food wasn't always fresh.

Abby finished wrapping the last cup and sighed. She could not get the picture of Luke's haunted face out of her mind. He had come for a final good-bye dinner the night before. His birthday was in ten days, but they would not be here for it. So her parents had suggested that she give him a pocketknife as a parting gift. Luke had smiled and hung it by its chain on his belt loop, then tucked it in his pocket.

But when the time had come to say good-bye, he had looked at Abby strangely, his eyebrows drawn into a line over his eyes. Abby remembered the cords in his neck bulging. Then he had simply bolted from the room.

"That's the last of the dishes, Ma," Abby said. Ma was watching her with concern.

"Thank you, dear." Ma tucked a stray lock of hair back in her bun and looked around the room. "I suppose we're ready to leave tomorrow morning."

Abby surveyed the trunk near the door and felt her hands begin to sweat. *How could this be happening?* she wondered for the hundredth time that day. The reality of leaving had driven the daydreams of adventure from her mind. *It's wrong to leave Luke behind!*

Earlier in the day, she had written a poem in her sketchbook about her mixed-up feelings. She wanted to share it with Luke.

"Can I ride over to Luke's now . . . to say good-bye?" Abby asked.

Ma's eyes softened with understanding. "Yes, please give him my love. We've already said our good-byes over dinner, but you should go visit one last time." Those words hung in the air like a swarm of deadly bees. Abby had to get out of the house.

"Be home before dark," Ma said as Abby draped her wool shawl around her and headed out the door. Her thoughts were already returning to the words of her poem for Luke:

> *If day became night and night turned to day,*
> *I'd be less confused about going away.*
> *For the moon would come out at break of day,*
> *And the stars would shine for children at*
> *play.*
> *All the creatures who roam the world at night,*
> *The bat and the owl would be blinded by*
> *light.*
> *Eyes might then hear and noses might taste,*
> *And leaving you behind would seem less of a*
> *waste.*

Luke sat alone in his favorite stand of alders, the roots of which extended into the brown creek. The water had risen since the recent rain. When the weather was warmer, this hole was a good place to fish. But his mind wasn't on fishing or the grove's wooded scent, which usually gave him pleasure. His brows were furrowed deeply, his cheeks pressed into his hands as he leaned forward on the granite rock.

Ever so slightly, his body rocked back and forth. Sparks lay beside him, waiting. But his master never spoke. When a groan erupted from Luke, Sparks's head came up. Then the dog whined and laid his head back down between his paws.

Luke was caught in a mess. Being pinned under a logjam in a rushing stream would have been easier to get out of, he decided. On the one hand, he loved his dog and didn't want to do anything to hurt him. Sparks had traveled west with him, had kept him going when his heart hurt so badly he didn't want to live anymore. Leaving Sparks behind would just about kill him.

Luke threw a pebble into the swirling water. *How can I stay with that heartless woman unless Abby and her family are here? They're the only ones who love me,* he thought. If it hadn't been for them, he would have left right after he first arrived. The thought of living without those four special people made his chest ache. A sharp physical pain surged up under his ribs and made it hard to breathe when he thought about losing them forever. Because surely, if they moved that far away, he'd lose them.

He had to do something, and he had to do it quickly.

He touched the collie's smooth head. Sparks's tail wagged like the metronome on his aunt's polished piano.

"I love you, boy," Luke said. A lump swelled up in his throat. He lay back on the rock and Sparks rose up on his haunches, then cradled his silky head on Luke's chest. The pain in Luke's ribs seemed to ease a bit, but so did a burst of tears.

A soul-rending cry echoed through the little glade of trees, momentarily drowning out the gurgling stream.

Disturbed, a barn owl flew off, his brown wings arching over Luke in a whir of feathers. Luke watched through blurred eyes.

Up above him rose the first star in the darkening twilight. That light reminded him of something, of someone—and a time when life had been steady and welcoming. When he thought home would be forever, right along with his parents' loving smiles. Suddenly he could see the patchwork apron tied around his mother's plump middle, the flour on hands and cheeks, her green eyes full of love as she looked at him. Luke recalled the scent of freshly baked bread, as warm as her neck when she leaned over to kiss him good night.

"Say your prayers, Son." Her voice filled his head, and anguish burst like a firecracker in his heart. It had been a long time since she'd reminded him. A long time since he'd seen her alive. Even longer since he'd prayed.

Darkness covered the last rays of the setting sun. Stars, like white knots in a black quilt, dotted the sky. Yet their diamond points weren't luminous enough to walk by. Night was closing in now, terrifying him. Which way should he go?

"I need a light, Ma," he begged, gripping Sparks around the neck. "I need a light to guide me."

When Pa came in for dinner on their last night in Pueblo de San Jose, the rest of the family was already seated at the table. After prayer, they ate their sandwiches off the clean wooden tabletop since the plates had been packed.

"Tell me, Princess, did you see Luke today?" Thomas asked his quiet older daughter.

Abby's blue eyes looked more solemn than usual. "No. His aunt said he'd gone hunting with Sparks. Maybe he'll come by to see us tomorrow morning before we leave."

"Possibly," Pa responded, "but that will be awfully early. We have to catch the ship in Alviso by 4:00 A.M."

Abby knew they would take the barge down the nearby Guadalupe River to Alviso, and from there they would sail into San Francisco Bay and the waiting Pacific Ocean. Then it was only a matter of weeks until they crossed the Pacific and settled in a new land. All her life she had dreamed of adventure. Now she didn't want any part of it.

Abby watched the sun sink behind the western mountains from her bedroom. It would be the last sunset she'd ever see from this home.

Seven hours later, Abby woke to her mother's gentle touch. She leapt out of bed.

"Has Luke come?" she asked as she slipped out of her nightclothes and into her underthings and brown wool dress.

"Not yet, dear."

Sarah complained about being rolled out of bed. "Too cold, Mama!" she said, stamping her foot. But as her mother helped her strip off her nightdress, she quit complaining and hurriedly dressed.

"I've packed our breakfast, and we can eat once we board the barge," Ma said.

George, one of Mr. Morgan's workers, drove up in the flatbed and helped Thomas load up the trunks in the predawn dark. In just a few minutes they would be piling in and moving away from home, Abby realized. She threw on her blue wool cloak and stepped out into the frosty October shadows.

Her eyes searched the road leading toward town. But no sounds of approaching horse hooves broke the morning stillness.

When the loading was finished, Thomas beckoned Sarah and lifted her up into the flatbed wagon, where she perched on a trunk.

"Ready for your adventure, Little Britches?" he teased.

"Yes, Pa!"

Ma came out then with a lantern in one hand. "Well, I've checked everything, and there isn't a thing we've left behind," she said, blowing out the lantern. She smiled as her large husband lifted her easily onto the front seat.

Nothing we've left behind! Abby thought in misery. *Only Luke!*

"Pa, I need to check something," Abby said as she ducked in the front door and hurried to her bedstead. She peered out the window that looked west toward town. No one moved on the road. He wasn't coming after all.

As she came out the door, she worked hard not to let the tears spill. Pa lifted her into the back of the buckboard and jumped into the front.

"Let's go, George," he said, eager like Sarah to be off on the adventure. George gently slapped the reins on the horses' rumps, and the wagon lurched forward.

Ma turned and reached for Abby's hand, squeezing it tightly. "I think it was too hard for Luke to have to say good-bye again," she said tenderly.

Abby nodded mutely. A lump had sprung up in her throat as tears trembled on her lower lashes. Her life was over. Nothing would ever be the same again. She was leaving behind her friends, her school, and her church. They were moving to some horrible island where she would be isolated on her uncle's miserable ranch. This was not how she and Luke had planned it! She watched the little house— and Luke somewhere in the distance—disappear into darkness.

Chapter Six

Abby stood clinging to the foremast of the 120-foot schooner, the *Intrepid*. The ship headed into a cold northeasterly wind, and each time she plunged into the trough of an incoming swell, water droplets jetted above the deck and moistened her face.

Abby's cheeks reddened in the gusts, and her hair froze into a chestnut banner behind her. Since rising that morning, she had discovered that she loved sailing. Wrapping her fingers around the rigging, she gazed out over the endless blue sea and sky. The schooner danced into the wind like an untamed pony.

"Yer a natural sailor," said Captain MacDonald, coming up behind her. "It's too bad the rest of yer family isn't." His thick Scottish brogue and the way he rolled his *r*s delighted Abby. How she wished her parents and Sarah could join them, but they were resting in their shared cabin below. In fact, out of the two families traveling onboard the ship, Abby was the only one who had showed up topside.

"They're a wee bit sick in the tummy, eh?" the captain asked.

Abby turned toward the white-haired, leather-skinned captain. "Yes, I'm afraid so. All but Pa—and he's taking care of Ma and Sarah."

"What calls yer family to Hawaii?" Captain MacDonald asked, taking the yellowed meerschaum pipe from between his lips.

"Hawaii?" Abby asked. "I thought it was named the Sandwich Islands. Luke always says the islands are famous for their ham sandwiches."

The captain laughed as he emptied the pipe over the side of the ship. "And who is this Luke?" he asked, rubbing his silver beard that grew on the sides of his face like thick pork chops.

"My best friend . . . in Pueblo de San Jose." She swallowed her brimming emotions and stared back out to sea. "My uncle is sick and needs our help. Pa hopes to buy into the ranch once we get there."

The captain gave her a knowing look. "It's hard to leave home, isn't it, lassie?" He went on without waiting for an answer. "But yer parents are doing the right thing; it's an effort to improve yer lot. Ah, 'tis a grand land yer sailing to!"

Abby smiled at his hopeful words.

"Come on, lass, I'll teach you how to steer my *Intrepid* lady." With that, the two of them moved away from the bow of the ship toward the aft (rear) quarters and the large oak steering wheel with spokes of polished wood.

"Take her like this, lassie," the captain said as he relieved the Hawaiian sailor on duty, "and hold her steady." He placed her hands on the wheel. It tugged against her grip as if it had a mind of its own, but Abby held firmly. Wonder filled her as she realized she was controlling the grand vessel. She could feel the push of the winds against the sails and the ocean surging against the wide rudder under the ship. She glanced over at Captain MacDonald and grinned. He smiled in understanding. Sailing could lift anyone's spirits.

The wind picked up momentarily. Abby heard it whistle through the shrouds. The wheel tugged a bit more, but she held the ship steady.

The captain nodded with satisfaction. "I'll be checking on the crew and leaving Mr. Lancaster in charge of the deck, now, lassie. Hold her steady for a few more minutes and then Kimo will take over," he said, referring to the previous steersman, a large, dark-skinned sailor in blue duck-cloth breeches and a white cotton shirt. A red kerchief tied around his neck served as a uniform of sorts. Kimo looked up from rope braiding and gave Abby a wide grin, revealing brilliant teeth.

Abby watched the captain make his way forward. His trim form in the navy wool suit with shiny brass buttons mirrored the way he ran his ship: with discipline. When they came aboard, the captain had told her that he ran a tight ship and tolerated no tomfoolery.

As Abby watched him pass the first mast, a sudden movement to the right caught her attention. The jollyboat, used for rowing to shore, sat above the deck, secured to the starboard bulkhead. Abby kept her hands firmly on the wheel as she looked the jollyboat over again. A gray tarpaulin snugly covered it. She could not figure out what movement had caught her attention.

Then she saw it. One corner of the tarp at the back of the boat was not snapped down. It caught and lifted in the breeze. *There it goes again,* she thought as the tarp flipped up. But this time it revealed a lock of sun-streaked hair followed by dark eyebrows and a familiar grin. Her eyes widened in shock.

Luke!

When she saw him wink, Abby gasped and instinctively let go of the wheel. The ship pitched hard to port. Kimo lurched toward her to catch the spinning wheel, but Abby quickly regained her hold of it.

As Kimo's strong arm came from behind her to steady the wheel, she glanced over her shoulder at him. His bronzed arm resembled a thick trunk of wood.

"Little missy make a messy!" he joked, then broke into a hearty laugh.

"I guess I did." Abby sneaked a peek at the jollyboat again. Luke wasn't there! Had she imagined it? Did she want to see him so badly that she had imagined seeing him?

"I take wheel for you now, little *wahine*," Kimo said. Abby gladly gave over the helm to him. She had to get away to think. Was Luke really there? She looked at the jollyboat again. Not even the tarpaulin moved now.

Abby headed toward the hatch for a few moments alone. As she neared the jollyboat, her heart pounded in her chest. Blood rushed through her ears. *Luke,* she wanted to yell, *are you really here?* But if he was, she could not give him away. Obviously, if she hadn't imagined it, Luke was a stowaway. That was a very serious offense, especially on a ship run by no-nonsense Captain MacDonald.

If Luke should be discovered before they put California far behind them, Captain MacDonald would turn the ship around and take him home, she was sure of it. *He must stay hidden! And I've got to do all I can to help him.* She bit her lower lip. *Oh, Luke, are you really here?*

Once her parents discovered him, they might worry about Luke's aunt. Still they would be glad to see him, too. She knew they loved him. But by the time they reached the islands, it would be too late and too costly to send him back!

Abby walked toward the jollyboat on the way to the hatch, sure that her plan would work. As she approached the boat, she slowed her gait, and her hand instinctively brushed the tarpaulin. It was all she could do to keep from giving him away in her excitement. *Oh, Luke!* her mind screamed. *You found a way!* She climbed through the hatch, eager to get to her sketchbook. She wanted to draw Luke's face right away, and she knew just the caption she'd write beneath it: *When one door closes, another one opens.*

Abby clutched her skirt as she tiptoed up the steps of the hatchway. As her head popped out of the hatch, she took a moment to get her bearings in the darkness.

It had taken hours for her parents to fall asleep. She had lain awake waiting. Once she heard her father's deep snores, she had hurried to dress and made her getaway. She just *had* to know if Luke was really there!

During the midnight watch, she suspected that only a few crew members would be on deck. She stepped onto the tilting deck and made her way, in her stocking feet, toward the jollyboat.

She could see two lanterns swinging in the rigging, fore and aft, at either end of the ship. Sitting near each was a sailor on watch. The one in the stern of the ship spoke quietly to the steersman. Abby ducked low as she crept forward.

When she reached the bulkhead where the jollyboat was fastened, she stood up and lifted the edge of the tarp. "Luke," she whispered. Her voice seemed to disappear amid the night breeze and the slap of seawater against the ship's hull.

Suddenly a rough hand covered Abby's mouth, and a strong arm grabbed her around her waist. Instinctively she kicked backwards, and her heel met with a shinbone. The hand flew off her mouth.

"Ouch!" Luke growled.

Abby pivoted toward him. First a smile broke across her face, then a look of alarm. "What are you doing out here?" she demanded fiercely.

Luke grabbed her arm and crouched low beside the bulkhead, drawing her down with him. "I couldn't take being cooped up anymore. Had to stretch my legs, but we've got to get back under-cover to talk." He lifted the unsnapped edges of the tarp. "Scoot in."

Abby gave him a hug, then glanced fore (to the front) and aft. The sailor on the bow stared straight out to sea. The other two were engrossed in their conversation. She wiped the sweat off her palms and crept up on the bulkhead and swung first one leg and then the other into the jollyboat. As she sat down and ducked her head under the tarp, she made room for Luke.

If Captain MacDonald discovers us, he'll consider this tomfoolery for sure!

Luke slid in beside her and exhaled in relief. After replacing the tarp, he faced Abby.

At first she could see nothing, but gradually her eyes adjusted to the dim light. She couldn't help grinning at Luke.

He smiled back. "We won't need a lantern—your smile's lighting up the night."

She laughed softly. "How'd you sneak onboard?" she asked. For hours she'd tried to imagine how he'd done it.

"Jacob and I rode Lightning to Alviso," he began. "I made Jacob promise not to tell a soul. Then he took the horse back to my aunt's stable for me, and I waited for a chance to board when no one was looking." He paused. "It took awhile."

He makes it sound so easy, Abby thought.

Luke sighed. "The hardest part was leaving Sparks. I . . . gave him to Jacob until I get back." His voice caught, as if he couldn't swallow. "He promised to be good to him."

Abby took Luke's hand. "He will." Then, in a soothing voice, she continued, "I'm glad you're here. You're part of our family. Ma and Pa will be happy to have you." She gave his hand a squeeze.

"I don't know, Abby. I've been laying here thinking about that. They might see fit to send me back . . . or maybe write my aunt." He was silent for a second; then his voice grew harsh. "I'm not going back! I'd rather take up a sailor's life than spend any more time in her house."

Abby chewed her lip. To choose the hard life of a sailor over living in his wealthy aunt's house showed just how bad things were. Everyone knew sailors worked long hours for little pay and didn't see their families for years at a time.

Why is life so unfair? Abby wondered. Luke had lost his family, and if things didn't go well with her parents, he would be forced into a lonely life at sea. They just *had* to take him once they reached the islands—there was no other choice. But would they?

"Did you pack any food?" Abby asked.

"Yep. A bag of apples, carrots, some beef jerky, and I sneaked two loaves of Maria's bread. Brought raisins, too." He paused. "But I already miss her chicken and biscuits!" His white teeth gleamed as he smiled.

She dug in her skirt pocket. "Here. I saved you some hardtack biscuits from our supper. They aren't too good, but they'll fill your belly."

Luke bit into one. "It tastes like tree bark, only harder," he said after chewing for a while. Abby chuckled.

"I better get back to my bunk before I'm missed," she whispered. "I'll try to bring you something from our dinner every night, all right?"

Luke nodded. "I especially need a jar of water."

"Of course." How stupid of her not to have thought of that! "Anything else?"

"Naw, just . . . thanks for coming, Ab." His loneliness seemed to fill the space around them.

Tears flooded Abby's eyes, but she knew Luke

couldn't see them in the dark. "This isn't exactly how we pictured our adventure, is it?"

In the stillness, she could hear him breathe. "No," he finally answered. "But I reckon we've got to be grateful for all we have. This isn't the worst life can hand you."

She swallowed hard, knowing he was thinking of his parents' deaths. "Luke, thanks . . . thanks for coming."

They sat together, listening to the waves splash against the hull and to the masts creak with the pitch and roll of the ship. They were comfortable in the silence as only good friends can be.

Finally, she pushed back the tarp. "Here I go." She climbed awkwardly out of the boat and crouched beside the bulkhead. Then she cautiously made her way back to her bunk.

Chapter Seven

Although they had been at sea for eight days, Abby worried. Had enough time passed for Luke to be safe from a return trip to his aunt's home?

Since discovering him, she had spent as much time as possible on deck each day, keeping an eye on the jollyboat. Fortunately, it seemed to be ignored by everyone.

But Luke was always on her mind. During every evening meal, she secretly slipped part of her supper into her pocket. Then, when only two sailors were on midwatch—between midnight and 4:00 A.M., she brought the food to Luke. Although her parents were always asleep, it was risky sneaking out on deck to bring a jar of cold water and whatever food she had saved for him.

But tonight she had not been able to save anything. The cook had not set out any of the hard-tack biscuits usually served with the evening meal. Worse yet, the dinner had been soup! So she had nothing to share with Luke.

Lord, Abby prayed as she sat up in her bunk, *help me figure out something for him. I know he's hungry.*

At least Luke had brought a little food with him, including a bag of fall apples from his aunt's orchard. Still, that was nothing compared with the passel of food she'd watched Luke put away after he worked alongside Pa. Abby thought of the heaping plates of fried potatoes, corn, green beans in bacon grease, ham, and the two pieces of apple pie he usually had during his meals at her house. Pa had always laughed and said he was the "growingest" boy he'd ever seen. Sometimes Luke had six cookies and a glass of milk to wash it all down, too!

Suddenly Abby sat up in bed. Sarah turned over in the dark, and Abby held her breath in hopes her sister hadn't disturbed their parents' sleep. *Cookies! We have a whole tin of molasses cookies, Luke's favorite, right here at the foot of my bed in Ma's carpetbag!*

She hated to take them without permission, but Luke's situation was desperate. If her mother knew, she'd gladly share them.

Abby crept out of bed and dressed quickly. Then she rummaged through her mother's carpetbag until she found the tin. Carefully opening the cabin door, she slipped out, glad that their cabin was close to the hatchway. She climbed up and spied around, like a prairie dog peering out of his hole in the ground. On either side of the *Intrepid* single lanterns hung, casting a pale light fore and aft. But the ship's midsection, the "waist," was cloaked in blackness.

Once on deck, Abby crouched low. By now she had her "sea legs," so her body instinctively adjusted to the slanted deck as she made her way to the jollyboat. Unsnapping the tarp on the back corner, she handed Luke the cookie tin and jar of water. Then she stepped in, scooting her legs under the wooden seat built into the skiff, and replaced the tarp.

Abby scrunched down on the hard wooden boat bottom and let her eyes adjust to the dark.

"Here. These are your favorite cookies—molasses," she offered brightly.

"You remembered my birthday," Luke said simply.

Abby was taken by surprise. Luke's birthday had completely flown out of her mind, what with the excitement of him being a stowaway. "Happy birthday," she said softly, grateful the Lord had answered her prayer by giving her the idea for the cookies on *this* night.

"Thanks," he returned, with a smile in his voice.

"So, what have you been doing?" Abby teased, knowing he had been doing the same thing as ever—lying still in cramped quarters.

Luke turned on his side and flicked her nose. She wrinkled it and stuck her tongue out at him.

"If you must know, I've been using that other

birthday present you gave me before we left California."

"The knife?"

"Yep, I brought some pine, and I've spent most of the day whittling."

"Let me see!"

Luke moved toward the bow of the boat and rustled around in a burlap sack. He inched back to Abby and handed her a piece of wood about a foot long. Abby ran her hands over the grainy surface of the wood. It was beginning to take shape.

"It looks like some type of four-legged creature," she said.

"You'll see." Luke grinned. "I think I'll keep it a mystery and see how long it takes you to figure it out."

Luke opened up the cookie tin and munched a soft molasses cookie. The dark sugar scent filled the enclosed space and made Abby's mouth water.

"Want one?" he asked.

"No." *Best keep every bite for him in the coming weeks,* she thought.

"In fact, I better get back," she said, raising her hand to move back the tarp.

Luke's hand shot up to stop her. "It's my birthday, Abby. Can't you stay a bit longer?"

She thought of how lonely and uncomfortable it must be for an active boy of fourteen to lie in the jollyboat day in and day out. Just as she was about to agree, a smell struck her nose. *Pipe tobacco!*

Abby placed one finger to her lips and laid one over Luke's, too. She shook her head no. The scent grew stronger, and Abby looked above her to see if the tarp was in place. One corner was ajar! *Captain MacDonald must be close by!* She froze, every muscle taut and tense.

Luke, too, held still, his face registering the seriousness of the situation. What would happen if they got caught? Was there a law about stowaways? Could he go to prison? Or be keelhauled? Everyone knew that law aboard ship was the captain's word and whim. Often those who disobeyed were lashed with a whip.

These thoughts were interrupted when Abby heard footsteps nearby, almost on them. Neither dared to breathe.

Then came a sound—*harrumph*—and a pair of hands fumbled with the edge of the tarp. Abby's eyes dilated with fear as she heard the snap being pushed into its metal socket.

Next Abby heard a tapping against wood and remembered how the captain emptied his pipe against the ship's outer hull. *He must be done with his pipe,* she reasoned, *and on his way back to bed.* She lay still awhile to be sure. But already the boat bottom had become uncomfortable. How awful this must be for Luke!

The ship's movements became hard to resist. Abby and Luke listened to waves sloshing rhythmically against the ship and the tackle above them creaking. In their self-imposed silence, they relaxed.

The danger had passed, and Abby simply had to wait a bit. She never noticed closing her eyes until she started when Luke nudged her.

"Don't fall asleep on me," he whispered.

"I wasn't asleep."

"You were for a second. I heard you snore."

"Then I've got to go! What if we'd both fallen asleep and day had dawned?"

Luke took a deep breath. "Thanks for the birthday party, Ab." She smiled and lifted the tarp.

Slipping through the darkness, Abby soundlessly made her way back through the hatchway. As she crawled gratefully into her berth, she remembered God's promise from the Old Testament that Ma had read before they left home: "I am with you and will watch over you wherever you go." Nestled amid her sleeping family, with Luke onboard too, that promise was now easier to believe.

While they were closer to California than Hawaii, the weather had remained cool. But after two weeks of steady wind, they had encountered the warmth of the South Pacific. The days had heated up; even Ma and Pa left their stuffy cabin to sit under the awning

Captain MacDonald had rigged for them. Ma was constantly calling Sarah back to her side, afraid she'd fall overboard. *Poor Luke, who sits baking under the tarp!* Abby thought. Because of the heat, he had begged her to bring two jars of water each night.

But ever since she'd briefly fallen asleep in the jollyboat, Abby had not climbed in to talk anymore. She knew Luke missed her, but it was more important that he make it safely undetected to Hawaii.

Two nights ago Luke had told her that his legs were cramped from not being used. "I'm determined to make it through," he had said. But the next night she had caught him walking on deck, stretching his stiff legs. "Luke!" she had whispered in fear. "You can't do this! What if someone sees you?"

"Abby, I've got to, or I won't even be able to sneak off this ship," he'd answered. And she'd realized he was right—he had to keep his legs limber. Soon they would be there, and she was glad because Luke was out of both apples and cookies. She had begun saving more from her own plate and often went to bed hungry now. It made it easier to stay awake with an empty stomach pinching uncomfortably. Recently Ma mentioned that Abby's dress was fitting more loosely. She noticed Ma was watching her more carefully during supper, and her watchfulness made it harder to sneak food into her pocket. *Oh, if only the trip would be over soon!*

Chapter Eight

Only two more days to go, Abby thought one afternoon as she sat learning how to tie nautical knots from Kimo, the big Hawaiian. She had already learned how to tie the bolan and the half hitch, but Kimo seemed intent on teaching her how to tie a rope bracelet like the one he wore.

"When we land in Oahu, I show you how to make plenty bracelets with puka shell," he said with a wink. "Then you look pretty, *wahine.* My mother, Olani, she teach you to make island lei, too."

Abby grinned at the offer. "I look forward to meeting her, Kimo. Is she as kind as you?"

The large man smiled proudly. "Olani is like goddess Peli, who spits fire from mountain. My mother is *ali'i,* from royal family. She big and beautiful, tall like me. But Olani wide." He stretched his arms out. "Like royal chieftess should be. Her hair like mountain mists, and sometime she spit fire, too." He laughed at his own joke. "You will know her. She live in Kailua, where your uncle live. Everyone there know Olani."

"It will be a real pleasure to know someone from the royal family," Abby said, her eyes shining. Since they sat on a bulkhead near the jollyboat, she hoped Luke could hear their conversation.

Kimo looked up to the east. "We be there quick, I think. I smell storm. We ride storm home." Abby's eyes followed his, but she could not see any sign of an approaching storm.

"Maybe," she said doubtfully.

Kimo grinned. "No maybe. It will come," he promised.

Abby bent over the rope and retied the knot she'd just let slip. She couldn't help but wonder, *If a big storm hits, will Luke be all right?*

The sky darkened early. By six, the usually balmy wind turned cold and the sky hovered overhead with black, threatening clouds. Captain MacDonald ordered the crew to trim the sails.

When the rain began, it was not a steady pattering of drops. It seemed a celestial floodgate had opened, and water sheeted down in liquid walls. While the sailors scurried for their oilskins, Captain

MacDonald ordered all passengers to stay belowdecks for the duration of the storm.

The one good thing about being cooped up in their tiny cabin was being able to eat there. Pa had gone to get the simple meal of hardtack biscuits and cheese and had distributed it to his family. Abby secreted two biscuits and a cheese chunk in her hanky under her pillow for Luke. Now as she and Sarah clung to their berth that night and tried to sleep, she hoped the storm would blow over before she had to go topside.

For three hours the *Intrepid* pitched and rolled like a bucking mule. Abby lay in bed, worrying about Luke. At least she had a warm bunk to toss in. He was being tossed about on the hard wooden planks of the jollyboat!

Finally, when the storm quieted briefly, Abby's parents and Sarah fell asleep. Then Abby climbed out of bed carefully and slipped into her blue chambray dress. It took a minute to locate her shoes. They had been tossed into different corners of the tiny cabin. Normally she went in her stocking feet, but with wet decks she decided to wear her boots. With her pockets full of biscuits and cheese, Abby left her cabin and started for the hatch. She could hear the rain pounding on the deck and knew she was bound to be drenched by the time she got to Luke's hideout.

As she opened the hatch, the cold wind whipped her hair across her face. Rain sloshed down on her head and poured down her neck. "Ugh!" she said, grimacing as she lurched onto the pitching deck.

The ship keeled over to starboard, and Abby skittered across the slippery deck toward the railing. She grabbed onto the rigging and held fast, watching the lanterns at either end of the ship swing wildly in the storm. Thunder boomed, and suddenly lightning split the sky with the jagged slash of a white-hot knife. Abby immediately ducked down to avoid being seen. She inched along the middle deck toward the jollyboat. The rain stung her face and soaked through her dress.

Just as she neared the skiff, another bolt of lightning hit the sea several hundred yards ahead. At the same moment, thunder boiled overhead with a deafening crash. Abby screamed, but her voice drowned in the howling wind and thunder.

When she reached the boat, she flipped up the corner of the tarp, then dropped in the jar of water and threw herself in after it. She landed on Luke, who cried, "Ouch!"

"It's terrifying out there!" Drenched and shaking, she clung to him.

"Abby, you shouldn't have come." He gingerly put his arm around her wet shoulders. "Don't try to go back in the storm right now. It's too dangerous. You could be washed overboard!"

"Don't worry. I'm not going anywhere. But you have to eat."

Thunder rumbled overhead. When lightning flashed, the brightness penetrated even the heavy tarp, and Abby watched Luke's face pale with fear.

The waves mounted and crashed over the *Intrepid*, tossing the ship like a cougar tosses a meadow mouse. Under the tarp, Abby and Luke clung to each other and the sides of the jollyboat, but they received a beating as they were thrown from side to side.

Though it had already raged for hours, the storm grew more furious. Towering waves crashed over the deck and dangerously tipped the ship. Abby slammed into Luke as the *Intrepid*'s bow disappeared under a wall of water, and the boat keeled over sharply. The starboard bulkhead, which the jollyboat fastened on to, submerged under the foaming sea.

Abby clutched Luke's shirt as the jollyboat lifted slightly, then dragged under the rushing water.

"Hang on, Abby!" Luke yelled. "If the tarp rips off, we could go into the water!"

Suddenly they heard the snap of one of the rusted brackets holding the jollyboat in place. The little boat swung outward at the bow in the mighty surge of water. Abby's breath caught as she heard the

stern bracket snap as well. Now free, the jollyboat
plunged into the storm-tossed sea!

As the little boat dove into the waves, the tarp
momentarily kept it from flooding and sinking.
But as the skiff resurfaced, the portion above Luke
ripped off, and he flew over the side as the jollyboat
tipped in the heaving waves.

Abby's hand, which had been clenching his shirt
in a death grip, refused to let go. She lunged to the
edge of the skiff, her arm dragged downward by his
weight.

"Luke!" she screamed, but the wind snatched her
words.

Luke's head disappeared underwater, and Abby
got a mouthful of ocean as the jollyboat tipped sideways. *It's going down!* she thought in horror. Still,
she did not let go of his shirt.

In a moment, Luke resurfaced. He grabbed the
side of the dunking skiff and hauled himself back
into it. Both of them lay gasping and soaked in the
water pouring into the bottom of the boat.

"We've got to start bailing," Luke choked as he
hauled up the bucket that had been tied inside the
stern.

In the midst of the black storm, the jollyboat
rode the rolling waves like a cork bobbing along a
white-water river. Abby sat beside Luke, but in the
dark she could barely make him out. She could just
see the movement of his arms as he began bailing.
Another wave hit the boat and slapped Abby in the

face. Her long hair dripped like wet laundry on a line, and her teeth chattered with the cold.

"Here, Abby," Luke ordered as he handed her the bucket, "bail, and you'll warm up." She took the wooden bucket and began to bail, dipping the bucket in the foot of water again and again and dumping it over the side. She bailed furiously for several minutes. But it didn't help. She shivered just as hard because it wasn't only the cold that made her shake.

Fear gripped her heart as she looked through the rain for the lanterns from the *Intrepid*. They were nowhere to be seen!

"Luke!" she gasped, dropping the bucket in panic. "We're alone!" *Alone and adrift on the huge Pacific Ocean!* Terror gripped her. She leaned against Luke's side for comfort, but when she felt him tremble, she began to cry. *Can we survive, Lord?*

Chapter Nine

Abby's arm shook as she handed Luke the empty bucket. It had grown so heavy in the last few minutes. She could not lift it one more time.

"I'll finish," he said. "There's not much water left."

The bobbing of the jollyboat had lessened since the storm had ended. Abby could see Luke outlined against the dark gray sky. The clouds were clearing. She could see some stars and a slight glow from the eastern horizon.

Luke threw out the last half-bucket of water and set the can back in the stern. "Hey, I almost forgot. There's a mast and sail stowed under the benches," he said. "When it gets light, I'll see if I can rig it up. Maybe the wind will carry us to land."

Abby heard the hopeful note in his voice. Luke always loved a challenge. He had the supreme confidence that he could get out of any jam. *I suppose that's because he's strong. His body has never failed him. But our only chance now depends on the right winds, on the very breath of God,* Abby thought. Then she realized with a start that she hadn't prayed yet. She had been too busy just surviving.

She shivered in the predawn breeze and wrapped her arms about her middle in an effort to warm up. Her blue chambray dress was still wet, although the breeze now blew a warm, tropical air on her.

Luke looked over from his seat in the stern and then joined her.

"Are you still cold?" he asked.

She nodded.

"Me, too," he said as he put his arm around her.

Abby gazed up into his green-and-gold-speckled eyes. "I guess if I had to be lost at sea," she said, "I couldn't have picked a better friend for it."

He smiled at her. "We're in it deep. But at least I'm not living with Aunt Dagmar."

Abby returned the smile for the first time in hours. "At least we're living, period."

Luke agreed.

"Would you . . . would you pray with me?" Abby asked.

He looked down at his hand. "You pray for both of us, all right?"

She sighed and closed her eyes. God had helped them stay in the skiff, but would He bring them safely to land? The ocean looked so big, and their situation seemed so overwhelming. For the first time in her life, Abby was separated from her ma and pa. She might not ever see her family again. Emotions clogged her throat.

The little boat rocked on the wide, wide sea surrounding them. She sat wishing for something to hang on to, for some anchor of safety. Her parents were miles away. With a shock, Abby saw how much she'd always depended on the security of their presence. *Why, I've always taken it for granted that they would be there to help out. And when they couldn't fix something, I've always let them pray for me. That means I've taken God for granted, too. But now God is the only One who can help me.* As that realization hit, words from her mother's past reading flooded through her mind: "He stilled the storm to a whisper, and the waves of the sea were hushed." It was the anchor in the wide loneliness Abby needed—for she could see that he'd stilled the storm.

Suddenly she knew what to pray. "Thank You, God, for helping us so far. Please get us to land soon. And don't let Ma and Pa worry too much. Amen."

Luke looked toward the east. "Sun's coming up. We'll be glad to have a piece of that old tarp with us today."

"Why's that?" Abby asked, stifling a yawn.

"The tropical sun burns deep. You'll need to cover your skin till it gets used to it." Luke bent down and inspected the circular groove in the bottom of the boat. "Now that it's getting lighter, I think I'll see to the mast and sail." He handed her the ripped tarp. "Why don't you wrap up in this and see if you can get some sleep? I'll take first watch."

Abby settled down in the bow of the boat. Her worry had lightened since she'd prayed.

Luke looked up at the small sail, stretched tightly against the sky. The mast had fit snugly into the groove made for it. It hadn't taken too long to rig the sail, a job that had come back to him from long ago when he had sailed on Quaker Lake with his pa.

By the time the sun spilled its honey light over the sleepy sea, the little jollyboat had captured a northeasterly wind. The boat scuttled along on the low swells. Whether or not they were heading toward a distant shore, Luke didn't know. But he hoped so.

He looked over at Abby, fast asleep and curled up in the bow. Her tea-colored hair blew softly over the white tarp. After his ma, Abby was the kindest person he'd ever known. She always thought about others. Sometimes she drove him nuts when she'd recite poetry or stop right in the middle of things to draw a picture. *But I guess that's what makes her Abby. In spite of her leg weakness, she's got spunk. If she'd let go when I went over the side of the skiff, I don't think I could have made it back in. The waves were too strong.*

He remembered how the waves almost sucked him out of her grasp. If they had, he would have eventually tired—and drowned in the stormy sea. He shuddered at the thought.

And that wasn't the first time she'd rescued him, he reflected. There'd been those first days in Pueblo de San Jose, right after he'd arrived from Pennsylvania. His aunt's hard heart and a bunch of new faces at school had overwhelmed him in his grief over losing his ma and pa. But then Abby turned her beaming smile on him. It was like this very morning's light after the storm, he thought, grinning as he looked down on her.

You don't know it, Abby Kendall, but I think you're pretty great for a girl.

"Abby."

Abby's eyes opened at the sound of Luke's voice. She saw the blue sky overhead and a white triangle sail pinned to it. She heard the *lap, lap, lap* of the waves against the boat's gunwales and felt the steady rocking of the boat.

Abby sighed in warm contentment and stretched. When she glanced over at Luke, she sat up in surprise. "What are you doing out in the open?" she asked. "Oh." The night's storm came flooding back to her. They were no longer on the *Intrepid* but lost at sea.

Luke's green eyes were laced with red lines. "I'm trying to keep our little vessel near the coast," he answered. "But I think the rudder might've been damaged when we went overboard." His hand rested on the tiller that guided the unseen rudder.

Abby's eyes followed his glance and she saw a green coastline to their left. "Oh, thank God! Luke, we're going to be all right!"

He smiled at her. "We need to beach somewhere so we can try to find water. And I'm dog-tired. I've got to lay down for a bit."

She saw the exhaustion in his face. "Can I take it for a while?"

"I don't think so. There's a strong current fighting this rudder. I'm using all my strength to hold her steady. But, luckily, we've got a good breeze pushing us forward. When we come on the next stretch of white sand, we'll try to land."

"All right," she agreed. Abby cautiously rose and moved toward him with the tarp. "You've let me rest in the shade. Now it's your turn to keep the sun off." She draped the tarp over his right shoulder, where his forearm was exposed to the sun. She could see the bright red tinge there.

"Thanks." Luke grinned. "I'm glad you got some rest."

"How long did I sleep?"

"A few hours, I think."

Abby glanced around. The sun overhead poured down on the deep. She could see light rays descending into the sapphire water below them. When she looked to her right, she gasped. Several miles away, another island rose majestically from the ocean. "Look! There's land in that direction, too."

Luke laughed. "I noticed. But I don't have a clue where we are."

"Remember Uncle Samuel sent us a map of the islands of Hawaii on the back of his letter?" Abby asked thoughtfully. "When we studied them the night you came for dinner, I noticed that most of the islands are miles apart. But Maui, Lanai, and Molokai make up a triangle because they're set close together. The island to our left must be one of them!"

"You're right." Luke gazed at the green island. "We were traveling toward Oahu, but the storm must have pushed us south."

Just then, Abby gasped. "Look, a beach up ahead!"

"Great," Luke said. But then he pointed the vessel seaward.

"You're heading out to sea!" she exclaimed.

"We have to head out in order to tack back toward shore," he explained.

In a few minutes, he tacked, and the boom on the skiff swung to starboard. The jollyboat sped over the swells toward the glistening beach. Abby leaned forward in anticipation. Would they find water or islanders to help? As they neared the beach, she noticed a lacy fringe of waves crossing the small bay toward which they aimed.

At the same moment, she heard Luke say, "Jehoshaphat!"

"What is it?" she asked, frowning.

"It looks like a reef. One of those coral reefs your uncle wrote about in his letters." As they drew near, they could see waves dancing over the top of the reef.

"Will the boat ride over it?" Abby asked. Her stomach grew taut with worry.

What if the boat capsized and threw them out? What if they were tossed onto the sharp coral, cut open, and became lunch for a big hungry reef shark?

"I dunno," Luke said, never taking his eyes off the approaching waves, which were heaving over the barrier. "But if the boat tips, be ready to dive over!"

There was no time to answer him, for the ocean suddenly swelled under them and lifted them into the churning waves. Abby gripped the gunwale and hung on. The little skiff lifted higher and ran with the wave. Just as she thought they were over it, the boat bottom crunched on the coral and was caught. The little vessel shuddered in the ocean surge.

"The rudder!" Luke said, his arm flailing back

and forth as he worked the tiller. "We've lost the rudder! The coral's knocked it clean off!"

As the next set of waves surged over the coral, the sea lifted the boat up and over the coral. The wind pushed against the sail and carried them swiftly toward the beach.

The white sand glowed brightly in the noonday sun. Farther up the beach, trees swayed in the trade winds. Abby remembered Uncle Samuel had called them coconut trees.

Then the skiff surged with the tide onto the sand, and Luke leapt out and pushed the gunwale, guiding the boat to higher ground. Abby jumped out after him. Even though her skirts clung to her in the knee-deep water, she helped push the skiff up higher onto the sand.

"We made it!" she yelled joyfully. Luke grinned along with her, and she noticed that he was swaying with the breeze, just like the trees. "You better lay down in the shade and get some rest," she said. "I'll take this watch." She retrieved the tarp from the boat and laid it under a coconut tree for him.

Luke mumbled thanks and fell asleep almost before his head touched the canvas.

Abby watched his hair blow in the trade winds. *He deserves a good rest,* she thought. *I hope he sleeps for a few hours.* Sitting beside him, she unlaced her ankle-high boots and removed them, along with her stockings. She wriggled her toes in the sugarlike sand.

Then she wandered back down to the water's edge. The ocean wasn't chilly as it was near California. In the shallows warm waves frothed over her feet. Her toes sank softly into the golden sand. She bent down and washed her face with the water and almost rinsed her mouth out with it, but then she remembered saltwater would make her even thirstier than she already was. The water jar had been somehow lost in the storm. *Maybe I can find a coconut and break it open. Uncle Samuel claims there's nothing sweeter than the milk of a ripe coconut.*

Abby felt a surge of hope. *We could live off coconuts, if we have to. Maybe we could repair the jollyboat, too. And somehow we'll find my family again!*

Chapter Ten

As Abby sat in the shade of the coconut palm, her skirt dried quickly—and stiffly—from the saltwater. Her hair, which had taken a good dousing from the rain and sea, hung in nutmeg ringlets down her back.

What a view she had! The ocean shone like an aquamarine jewel, and the sky mirrored its hues with added wisps of distant white clouds. The soft paper sound of coconut palms rubbing against each other in the trade winds could have lulled her to sleep, but she knew she needed to look for fallen coconuts and a source of fresh water. Her tongue felt thick with thirst.

Abby turned and viewed the wooded area beyond the beach. She decided to venture there barefoot to give her boots time to dry. She stood and gazed fondly down at Luke. Hoping he would sleep soundly until she got back, she headed into the wooded area.

Some of the trees looked gnarled and dry,

while others were lush and green with a beautiful white-and-yellow flower that filled the air with a delightful, sweet fragrance. Abby picked a few, recalling that Uncle Samuel had once sent her some of the blossoms in a letter. She remembered his words: "Plumeria blossoms are often used to make flower leis, which islanders wear for special occasions."

"Ouch!" Abby jumped as a sharp thorn pierced her bare foot. The needle was an inch long and as hard as a nail. "Kiave!" she muttered as she sat down to pull the thorn from her foot. She was thankful it had not gone in far. She knew from Uncle Samuel that kiave trees were not native but had been imported to the islands. Their thorns had pierced many bare feet in the past twenty years—hers included!

Up ahead, Abby saw a coconut on the ground. But as she neared it, she heard a stream gurgling twenty feet away. She pressed on to the delicious promise of water.

She hiked her skirt to her knees and bent down to drink the cool, clear water. Never had it tasted so good! For several minutes she drank her fill, until she heard splashing nearby. As she raised her head, she saw a pair of legs standing before her in the ankle-deep stream. For a moment she stared at nut-brown, wrinkled knees.

Her mouth popped open as she raised her eyes. There before her stood an old Hawaiian man staring down at her with shadowed eyes and a scowl on his dusky face.

Abby's heart pounded as she stood up. Water dripped off her chin and she swallowed hard. "Uh, hello," she said uncertainly, trying to smile.

He did not return her smile. The scowl on his face deepened, revealing frown lines etched in his forehead and cheeks.

"*Haole* girl, why you here?" he asked.

Abby swallowed. "We . . . my friend and I came ashore in our skiff down there," she said, turning to point toward the distant sea. "He's . . . still sleeping there. . . . We were lost at sea."

The old man jutted out his chin. His dark eyes peered into hers, as if testing her soul. "Go back!" he said darkly, raising his walking stick and pointing seaward.

"Grandfather!" A girl's voice carried from a nearby grove of trees across the stream. Abby looked up to see a girl about her age emerge from a stand of plumeria trees. She was beautiful, Abby thought. Her long black hair hung down to her knees. "Grandfather, do not scare *haole* girl. She need our help." She walked toward them, her long hair swaying in the breeze and brushing the hem of her knee-length Hawaiian dress. The red wrap-around dress was sleeveless and tied in some fashion over her chest. A thick lei of white plumeria blossoms hung around her neck and a bright red hibiscus flower was tucked behind her left ear.

"I am Nalani," she said, smiling. "This be my grandfather, Lonokai. He a wise *kahuna*. In your language that means 'priest'."

As Nalani came near, she reached out and touched one of Abby's ringlets. "Your light hair like the color of coconut shell."

Abby laughed. "It sure feels like wood at the moment!"

Nalani took off her lei. Reverently she lifted the lei over Abby's head and laid it on her shoulders. "*Aloha*. Welcome to Maui," she said. "Here may you find all you need."

"Maui . . . we are far from Oahu, then?" Abby asked.

"Yes. Your boat will take you?"

Abby frowned. "No, no. It is too small. And it was damaged when we came to shore. We are glad to have made it here."

"Ahhh." Nalani nodded. "Then you go for Lahaina and meet sailorman for to take you."

Abby's face brightened. "Is this La . . . Lahaina close by?"

"Yes." Nalani held out her hand to Abby. "First, you come eat. Then you go for Lahaina. We treat you good." Nalani led Abby toward the grove of trees from which she had emerged.

At the mention of food, Abby's stomach rumbled. Nalani burst out laughing. "See, Nalani knows what good. You come, try *poi*. It a treat!" she said, beaming.

Following willingly, Abby glanced behind them.

Lonokai still scowled at her as he stepped behind them.

As they passed into the wooded grove, Abby saw up ahead a Hawaiian village. Eight grass huts were set in a circle with firepits in front of each. People milled around in the afternoon sun. Children squealed and played a running game that looked like tag. Two women sat near a hollowed-out stone, pounding something with a small club. A few old men sat in a circle, chatting. Lonokai went to join them.

As Abby emerged into the clearing, the activity stopped and all eyes focused on her.

Nalani pointed to her. "This be Abby. She needs food. Her boat was lost in great ocean."

Suddenly Abby was surrounded by at least twenty people, smiling and talking in broken English with strange Hawaiian words thrown in. She sat on the mat they offered.

One woman came toward her with a bowl of food, parting the crowd surrounding Abby. She held out the bowl. "*Poi,*" she said encouragingly. "You eat, feel good."

Abby took the bowl. "Thank you." When she looked down, however, she realized the food was unlike anything she had ever seen before. It looked like purple paste! *How can I eat this without a spoon?* she wondered.

Seeing Abby's confusion, the woman took back the bowl. She checked to make sure Abby was watching, then she dipped in her first two fingers, coating them with the purple paste, and stuck them in her mouth. Her eyes closed in obvious ecstasy as she licked every drop of *poi* from her fingers.

Abby gawked. *It must taste delicious.*

The woman urged her to try it. "Eat, eat!"

Nervously holding the bowl in her left hand, Abby plunged two fingers into the purple mush. Sure enough, it stuck like paste and coated her fingers. Abby looked at all the watching eyes as she cautiously stuck her fingers in her mouth. *Ugh! It's like sour mush—and feels like pond slime!*

The crowd held its breath, waiting for her reaction. When she smiled, heads nodded in appreciation. "Thank you," Abby said, gagging it down for the sake of politeness. She definitely would not pick it to eat, but since she was so hungry, she was also thankful.

When another older woman brought over a platter of fruit, she gladly took a banana and enjoyed every bite. Others came up to her then, offering her sliced papaya and cooked ham. Half a coconut was passed to her. Abby tipped it to her lips and drank its sweet, milky-white liquid.

All the while, Nalani sat close by and kept up a running conversation. "Do not worry about Lonokai, my grandfather. He remembers old gods, but the Queen Regent, Kaahumanu, threw them into sea. Now I follow white man's God. But Grandfather not trust *haole* people. He old man with old gods. He see many friends die for disease that come with *haoles*. But he forget the way of *aloha* . . . it is to welcome everyone."

Abby beamed at Nalani, grateful she explained why her grandfather had scowled at her. "You're very kind, Nalani. Thanks for the food, but I think I should get back to Luke now before he wakes up."

"Who is Luke?"

"My friend. He's sleeping on the beach. We were thrown overboard during a storm. Now we need to find my parents on Oahu . . . somehow," she explained. A knot constricted in Abby's throat. They were so far away from home, so far away from her parents. How could they get a ride on a ship to Oahu when they had no money for passage? *What if I never get back to my parents?*

Nalani's eyes glistened with compassion. "You get home. In Lahaina be plenty sailors and ships. You watch out for bad sailors. They drink too much rum and fight at night." Nalani brushed her long hair back and put her finger on her lips, as if deep in thought. "I know!" she said brightly. "You find sailors' pastor at white church near harbor. He help all *haoles* and pray big prayers."

"The sailors' pastor . . . that's wonderful, Nalani. Thank you. Now I must get back to Luke before he wakes and worries about me."

"Come," Nalani said, taking Abby's hand, "we bring him feast."

"And a bucket of water, too!" Abby said.

Luke smelled it in his sleep. *Ham . . . sweet potatoes . . .* , he thought as he began to wake and roll over, his eyes still closed. When his hand touched warm sand, his eyes flew open in surprise. Above him, Abby stood grinning. Right next to her stood a girl about the same age with long dark hair. She was an islander, dressed in a red-print shift, which only came to her knees.

Luke bolted up and stood gaping at Nalani. He'd never seen a female's legs before! Looking over at Abby, who had begun laughing out loud, he whispered, "An islander!"

He waited for Abby to introduce him, but she was laughing too hard, so Nalani stepped forward.

"*Aloha*, Luke. Welcome you to Maui. I am Nalani." Then she took the plumeria lei that was draped over her arm and placed it over Luke's head. She leaned forward and kissed him on both cheeks, which now glowed bright red.

Swallowing hard, he managed to get out, "Nice to meet you, I'm sure." Then he quickly looked away from Nalani's interesting island dress.

Abby quieted down enough to point to the food lying in bowls a few feet away. "Look, Nalani brought you food. It's real good, Luke. Eat, eat!"

Luke grinned at Nalani. "Thanks. You don't have to tell me twice!" Then he sat down in front of the bowls and, after a long drink of water, began a feast of roasted pig, bananas, baked breadfruit, and papaya.

"Here, try this one," Abby said, handing him a bowl.

He peered down. "It's purple, Ab. What is it?"

"*Poi*." Abby's eyes crinkled with mirth.

Nalani said encouragingly, "A treat. It made from taro." She dipped two fingers in to show Luke how it was eaten. She daintily stuck both fingers in her mouth, and when she pulled them out, they were clean.

Luke cautiously imitated her, dipping two fingers into the *poi*. As his fingers emerged, licked clean from his mouth, Luke's eyes narrowed with the shock of the vinegary flavor. "Mmmhhmm," he said noncommittally. "Very interesting."

"Yes, isn't it?" Abby added mischievously.

Nalani chuckled, apparently pleased that Luke enjoyed *poi* as much as Abby.

The girls watched Luke stuff himself for a few minutes, but when it appeared he planned to eat everything available, Abby grew bored. "Let's take a walk, Nalani," Abby invited as she headed toward the water's edge. "He's been hungry a *really* long time. You see, he was a stowaway on the ship, so he didn't get much food." She stooped and picked up a large pink shell on the beach.

"What is stow-way?" Nalani asked, her brown eyes serious. "A sickness?"

Abby examined the shell in her hands. "No, it means he hid on the ship so he could come along with us. No one else knew he was there but me."

"Ah. Your mother and father will take him in?"

Abby bit her lower lip. "I know they love him, and I think they'll take him in. He's like a son to them, but Luke's aunt is another problem. She's real rich and might try to get him back. I just don't know how it's going to work out yet."

Nalani stopped walking and shielded her eyes from the sun as she spoke to Abby. "You tell Luke, come live here. Our house big. Our hearts *nui*—big room for love."

"Thank you, Nalani. I will." Abby started back up the little dune to Luke then. She knew Nalani meant it with all her heart, but she wondered what Nalani's grandfather would say about a *haole* boy sharing their home.

Luke was lying on his back when they trudged up the short dune to him. Empty bowls were strewn about. "Ahh," he moaned with one hand on his stomach. "It hurts, Ab."

Abby gasped. "Luke, you ate *everything*?" She sat next to him on the warm sand.

"Do you think I overdid it? I mean, beings as how my stomach had probably shrunk some?"

She shook her head with a giggle. "Yes, but I think you'll live through it. I see you took a liking to the *poi*, too."

Luke burped and rolled over. "Oh, don't remind me. It was so purple."

"*Haole* boy eat good! I get more *poi*," Nalani said, gathering up the bowls, satisfaction spreading across her face.

With a full stomach, Luke fell back to sleep almost immediately. Abby helped Nalani take the dishes back to her grass home after washing them in the creek. With directions from Nalani, Abby learned they could follow the track that ran along the ocean until they got to Lahaina, the whaling capital of the Hawaiian Islands.

"Leave soon, so you be there not at night," Nalani warned. "Sailors drink rum too much. The sailors' pastor say grog is 'devil brew.' Better *haole* girls stay in then."

After many thanks, Abby left the little village and went back to watch over Luke. He had worked so hard to get them safely to shore that she couldn't bear to wake him. Finally she lay down on the sand, listening to the sound of the gentle waves lapping the shore. Above them, palm branches fluttered in the soft breeze, and without realizing it, she drifted off to sleep.

Chapter Eleven

"Abby!"

She could hear Luke's voice and feel him shaking her shoulder. Abby tried to flip over and pull the covers up, but there weren't any. Sitting up, she rubbed her eyes and yawned. "What time is it?" she asked.

"I dunno. But the sun's getting low in the sky, and we best git too." Luke rubbed his tummy, which bulged out more than Abby had ever seen it before.

She wearily rose from the sand and brushed off her stiff dress, thinking how much she'd like a hot bath and her own bed—even the narrow bunk she and Sarah had shared on the ship. *Will I ever see her again?* The question made Abby tear up, so she hid her face from Luke and bent to retrieve the basket Nalani had given her for their trip to Lahaina.

"We, ah . . . better hurry. Nalani says it's not a good idea to be on the Lahaina streets at night."

Luke glanced at the western horizon. "I'd say we have a couple of hours then. Let's get going."

They headed back toward the village and stopped for a drink at the creek. Abby showed Luke the path Nalani had pointed out to her. "We just stay on the path along the coast, and we'll be there soon."

Trees along the dirt path kept the cool ocean trade winds from reaching them. Sweat trickled down Abby's face in the tropical heat. "I'm tempted to tear these long sleeves off," she muttered to no one in particular.

"Why don't you ask Nalani to loan you one of her dresses?" Luke teased.

Abby's face was already flushed. There was no more room for a blush. "Very funny. For your information, I thought her native dress was lovely. In fact, it's sensible in this horrid heat."

Her eyebrows drew together as Luke hooted. "Oh sure," he said, "it's *lovely*—especially her unusual hemline!"

Abby ignored Luke and concentrated on the surrounding scenery. The air held the sweet scent of plumeria. Here and there she saw papaya trees and low bushes with large red hibiscus flowers.

But soon her legs grew weary, and her feet began to ache. When they reached a clearing, she wandered to the edge of a small cliff where the ocean surged against lava rocks below. Sitting down, she grabbed from the basket a jar of water Nalani had given them and took a sip.

Luke can go on without me, she thought. She didn't care for his attitude anyway. She felt tired, grumpy, rumpled, and hot. She was lost on an island in the middle of the Pacific Ocean without a way back to her parents. This was not the time for him to get sassy. He should know better.

"Come on, Abby," Luke called from behind her. "Don't take all day. What are you doing, drawing a picture?"

She would not turn around.

Truth was, her legs were too tired from walking. They'd only been on the trail forty-five minutes or so, but she was exhausted clean through. Luke usually understood that.

Abby finally stood. "I'm coming." Her voice sounded irritated, she realized, as she put the jar away and trudged back to the dirt path with its moist warm air.

"Let me take the basket," Luke offered, reaching for it. "Now let's git."

Another half an hour and Abby's ankles and feet began to go numb. Somehow they seemed to have a mind of their own, and they apparently liked tripping. She'd already fallen twice, bruising the palms of her hands. Finally, in frustration, she sat on a fallen log. "I've got to rest, Luke." He'd understand, she knew. He always had.

"No, we haven't got time to sit around. This is one time I have to push you, Ab," he said, drawing close to her. "Come on."

Her mouth dropped open and new beads of sweat appeared on her upper lip. Never in her life had Luke been so insensitive!

"What? Well, if you want me to press on so all-fired bad, go get me a horse!"

"Don't act like a stupid girl! Nalani's the one who told you to hurry."

"Oh, well—I'm sure sorry I let you sleep then. If I'd known you were going to act like a pigheaded boy, I wouldn't have." She crossed her arms and showed him her back.

Luke let out a frustrated growl and sat on a nearby boulder. "Never thought I'd see the day . . . ," he murmured loud enough for Abby to hear.

"I never thought I would either!" she shot back. She was furious at his unkind attitude. "You're rude and . . . and hardhearted and . . ." She bit her lip and glared toward the sea.

When Luke stayed quiet, Abby took a peek at him. He sat with shoulders hunched, head in his hands, looking utterly dejected. He sighed deeply and looked up. Their eyes locked, hers angry and stormy, his wet and full of some deep sadness.

"Don't you see, Ab, it's all my fault you're here. If I hadn't stowed away, you wouldn't have been out in the skiff during the storm. You'd be with your ma and pa now. It's my fault they're probably grieving their hearts out. They think you're dead."

Tears leaked out of the corner of one eye. It was the first time she'd ever seen Luke cry. She got up and came toward him. "It's not your fault, Luke. I'd do it all over again so you could live with us in Hawaii." She patted his back gently. "Thanks for worrying about Ma and Pa. I've been . . . worried too." Long-bottled-up tears spilled down her cheeks, too. She knew part of her sadness came from sheer exhaustion. She just couldn't walk as far as most people. She was physically limited, and it hurt to face that fact.

Luke gripped her hand and urged her to sit next to him. His arm came around her shoulder. "We're a fine pair of blubbering babies, aren't we?"

Her face brightened. "No—just best friends."

He hugged her. "Best friends on their way home."

Abby bent down and retrieved a thin stick. Winding her hair into a coil at the nape of her neck, she stuck the stick through it. "There, that should be cooler. I'm rested now, Luke. Let's get to Lahaina and the sailors' pastor."

"Give me a second." He rummaged in the basket, taking out a little wooden bowl covered with a red cloth. "I could eat again. What's in here?" he asked as he removed the cloth.

Abby bit her lip. "Nalani packed your favorite— *poi*."

Grimacing, Luke placed the bowl on the rock. "She's a thoughtful girl, but maybe some nearby beast is starving. Let's leave it right here, just to be nice."

Abby's laughter rang out as the two started down the path and the sun dipped below the horizon.

Abby and Luke walked slowly in the darkening gloom. Tree roots seemed to lunge up out of the pathway, tripping Abby often. Luke grabbed her twice before she went down again.

As their path drew them along the ocean, they stopped to watch the silver-tipped waves break on shore. The air was balmy. When the moon emerged above the horizon, it cut a shining path over the black sea toward them. On the beach, sea crabs scuttled up and down the sand, scavenging for food.

"Look, Ab," Luke said, pointing down the curve of the bay. "I can see the lights of the town up ahead. We ought to be there pretty soon."

Abby followed the direction of his finger. "Great. Let's go."

"That's the way," Luke said.

Half an hour later, the two found themselves on the outskirts of Lahaina. Palm, mango, and plumeria trees grew thickly around the many fish ponds and watered gardens of the town. Low stone walls bordered crops.

"Look." Luke indicated a stream running across their path. "There must be a freshwater spring up in the hills behind the town. They're using it to water their crops."

Abby could see the moonlight reflecting on the surface of the many ponds and wetlands. Luke stepped up on a thick rock wall. "Let's walk on this stone pathway," he suggested. "We'll keep our feet dry." He helped Abby up onto it. The rock fence brought them to the edge of Lahaina.

Even before they entered the town, they could hear piano music escaping through the open doors of the grogshops on the street that fronted the ocean. Rowdy sailors congregated on the wooden walkway before the shops and saloons. Whale-oil street lamps gave light to walk by as Abby and Luke gingerly made their way down Front Street, as the signpost claimed.

To their right, the ocean continued to sweep toward the storefronts, but the waves only pounded in frustration against a rock seawall. Abby had the impression the ocean wanted to surge in and wipe away all the loud, gambling sailors from the quaint seaport.

She and Luke walked with their shoulders touching as they moved down the street away from the saloons and close to the seawall. Out in the bay, a fleet of whaling ships was anchored, awaiting the return of their rowdy crewmen.

"So this is Lahaina," Abby said.

Luke brushed his hair off his sweaty forehead to catch the cool trade winds blowing off the water.

"Yep. We're entering the whaling capital of the world. Not hard to believe by the look of all those ships out there."

Abby's eyes raced ahead of her as she read the signs of other establishments on Front Street: *The Mercantile, Won Ton's Chinese Apothecary, The Cooperage* (where barrels were made), and *Tucker's Sail Repairs.* But by far, all shops were outnumbered two to one by the many saloons with descriptive names, such as *The Scotsman's Lair, The Rum Barrel,* and *Grog & Gambling.* As the two passed each one, they could hear the tinkling of glasses, and sometimes angry voices.

Just as they neared the end of the street, which was taking them toward a large inn fronting the harbor, two burly men crashed through the doors of one grogshop, landing on the dirt street right in front of Abby and Luke. The fall to earth didn't even slow the two men as they rolled to their feet and circled each other with raised fists. Luke took hold of Abby's hand, moving himself ahead of her slightly as they watched the unfolding drama with open mouths.

"Ye had it comin', ye yello' bellied snake. No one calls me mother a name and lives to tell about it!" The angry sailor stood in the dirt street with his booted feet wide apart and his shirtsleeves rolled up high, revealing massive biceps. He jabbed with his right, catching the taller man on the chin. Abby shuddered at the sound of fist crashing into jawbone.

The taller man twirled when the blow caught him but returned to catch his assailant on his blackbearded chin. Again and again, the two fists collided with each opponent's face until, several minutes later, the tall, thin man lay sprawled in the street, apparently unable to rise for any more punishment.

The muscle-bound sailor in the tight shirtsleeves stood above him and grabbed a shock of the man's hair. Slipping his dagger from its sheath, he held it to the fallen man's throat. "Take back what ye said, or I'll slice yer throat like my mornin' papaya."

Almost unconscious, the other man murmured, "I take it back, Jackal." The victor sheathed his knife, dropped the man's head back onto the street, and began to walk away.

Abby's hands unclenched as relief poured through her. But suddenly Jackal pivoted and stomped back to the fallen sailor. He brought back his booted foot and kicked it forcefully into the man's side. "That'll help ye remember me in the mornin'!" he said with a wicked laugh. Abby gasped at the sight, and only then did he look in their direction. Luke stepped in front of Abby to shield her as the victorious sailor stalked toward them.

His wild black hair had come loose from the thong that had tied it back. As he opened his mouth to speak, his black beard jutted forward. "What be ye lookin' at?" Jackal growled. His pointed incisor teeth looked menacing, like fangs.

"Nothing, sir," Luke said quickly.

The sailor eyed them up and down with disgust. "Then shut yer hangin' traps and be off!" he yelled. Luke's eyes filled with fear as he pulled Abby along, and they hurried away from the scene. Behind them, they could hear the sailor's harsh laughter. Goose bumps rose up Abby's arms as she and Luke rushed along Front Street toward the little harbor up ahead. For as long as she lived, she'd never forget the sound of Jackal's vicious cackle.

When they passed the last shop and street lamp, Abby spoke up for the first time since witnessing the fight. "I've never seen anything like that, Luke! Never seen anyone who looked so cruel! He was just like that famous pirate, Blackbeard!"

Luke's nose wrinkled in disgust. "He wasn't exactly the ladies' welcoming committee, was he?"

Abby tried to shake off her feelings of unease. "Nalani said the little white church was on the other side of the harbor."

"There it is," Luke said. In the shadows of a tall banyan tree stood a little church with a small steeple and narrow steps leading up to the front door. As they neared it, they could see that the door stood open.

Luke still gripped Abby's hand. "Let's see if the sailors' pastor is in."

Still unnerved by the wild man she would always think of as Blackbeard, Abby almost whimpered. "Let's hope the pastor's here. This town surely needs one!"

Chapter Twelve

As they climbed the stairs, Abby could hear soft voices coming from inside the little church.

"Luke, I think he's here!"

"Shhh." Luke poked his head inside the door and peered into the candlelit room. "There are two men up front. Let's wait till they're done."

Luke sat down on the stairs, but Abby peered into the church. She could see a large wooden cross on the wall behind the altar. Wooden pews filled the room, except for the center aisle. Sitting on the first pew was someone who appeared to be the pastor with another man—a sailor, Abby guessed. Their heads were bowed in prayer, but Abby couldn't make out their words. She returned to sit with Luke.

"It looks like he keeps the church open late at night to help repentant sailors," she said. Somehow, being at this church reminded her of her own church back home, where she felt safe, loved, and close to her family. A lonely ache shivered through her. "I bet he's a wonderful pastor."

"I suppose," Luke said noncommittally. "Seems like a hopeless job with all those grogshops just down the street. I sure don't see sailors lined up at his door."

Abby sniffed. "Well, if even one sinner repents, the angels in heaven rejoice!"

"Is that so?" Luke drawled. "I didn't know angels went to parties. Next you're going to tell me they dance?"

"They'd probably hold a ball if you were to repent, Luke Quiggley!"

Luke smirked at her in the moonlight. "Well, don't hold your breath. I ain't a dancer or a believer."

Abby turned away. "I know." She hadn't been much of one either, she realized.

Her quiet words bothered him more than he cared to admit. "Aw, don't be so glum. If there is a God, then He's probably got a plan for hopeless cases like me."

Just then they heard footsteps behind them. When they turned, they saw two men exiting the small church. Luke jumped up and held out his hand to the man dressed in a pastor's white collar. "Hello, sir. I'm Luke Quiggley, and this here is Abby—Abigail Kendall. We've come to see if you can help us."

The pastor shook Luke's hand and nodded at Abby as she rose to greet him. "I'm Pastor Achilles, but everyone around here knows me as the sailors' pastor. I'm pleased to meet you both." Then he shook hands with the man who stood beside him. "Charlie, don't forget to read your Bible every day. It'll fill you with living water, and you'll have no need to drink the whiskey again."

The grizzly-faced sailor gave him a parting grin. "Thanks for the Book, Pastor," he said, holding the Bible up as he headed down the steps.

Pastor Achilles addressed Abby and Luke. "Now young ones, what can I help you with? Have you come to learn of God?"

Luke cleared his throat. "No sir. Abby, here, was raised in church. The help we need is a little more practical."

Abby jumped into the conversation. "We were lost at sea in the ship's jollyboat, and my parents probably think we've drowned. But of course, we haven't. All the same, we need to get to the island they're on in order to tell them!"

The pastor's mouth opened in surprise at Abby's frantic explanation. Then he put one arm around each of them, shepherding Abby and Luke through the doorway into the church. "Why don't you come in and tell me about it—I mean, from the beginning."

Abby took a breath of relief. They had found the right man to help them, she was sure. They only had to explain their situation, and he would find them a sea captain heading to Oahu.

As they settled themselves in a pew near the candlelight, Abby said, "Well, it began a few weeks back in California when my parents received a letter from Uncle Samuel. . . ."

Half an hour later, the pastor rose stiffly from the hard bench and rubbed his clean-shaven chin. "I think I know just the man to help you—Captain Horatio Chandler. I led his son to Jesus last year before the poor lad shipped to Brazil and died of the fever. Broke the captain's heart, but he's a good man, and I'm sure he'll help you. If I'm not mistaken, he's bound for Oahu—perhaps even this very night with the rising tide. We'd best hurry and see if we can locate him in town. Otherwise, we'll have to swim out to his ship—something I hate to do at night. One never knows what's lurking in the dark below one's legs!"

Luke arched his eyebrows at Abby. "Hurry up, Ab. I don't aim to go swimming when the sharks are out looking for dinner."

The two quickened their steps as they followed Pastor Achilles away from the peaceful little church and back into the noisy streets of Lahaina.

Pastor Achilles led them along the wooden boardwalk of Front Street, stopping to peer in each saloon. When he disappeared inside the *Grog & Gambling* and was gone more than a few minutes,

Abby's curiosity nagged her. Luke sat patiently on the boardwalk with his back to her, but she just had to peek inside.

She slipped through the open door and stood, searching the room. Although it was smoky inside, candles on tables lit the interior well enough for Abby to see. The sounds of glasses tinkling, sailors talking, and chairs scraping the floor filled her ears as she peered through the dim light in search of Pastor Achilles.

"Ha-ha-ha!"

Abby stiffened as rough laughter rang in her ears. She knew that laugh—and it made her wince in fear. Her pulse picked up, thrumming in her temples. It was the evil laugh of the sailor with whom she'd so recently come face-to-face!

Searching through the gloom, Abby saw him sitting with another man at a table in the back of the tavern.

"To success!" He raised his rum glass and clinked it against his drinking partner's. After downing the drink, he rolled up a piece of leather and slipped it inside his shirtfront.

But as he took another swig of grog, his eyes roved beyond his drinking partner and fell on Abby. His smile died instantly, revealing a chilling expression that made Abby swallow nervously. Instinctively, she inched back toward the wall, gasping when her hands bumped into it.

Still looking intently at her, the sailor began to

rise. When his chair fell over and he didn't stop to right it, Abby panicked. He was striding toward her!

Oh, no! Her legs felt like jelly. She stood rooted to the spot as the sailor, his hand resting on the hilt of his dagger, came closer and closer through the crowd and noise.

"Abby?" It was Pastor Achilles' voice suddenly beside her. "This is Captain Horatio Chandler of the *Flying Lady*."

Abby eyed the pastor gratefully and held out a limp hand to the blue-coated captain. "Hello, sir."

"As it happens, he and his crew are leaving tonight for Honolulu." The pastor smiled. "Good news, eh?"

Captain Chandler stood straight and tall in his coat with brass buttons. His hat was off and tucked under his left arm, revealing dark-brown hair with a streak of gray at each temple. He extended his right hand to shake hers. "Always glad to help a damsel in distress," he said with a conspiratorial wink. "But I thought you had a traveling companion."

Abby's eyes darted back to the sailor. He'd stopped dead in his tracks, but his eyes focused on her. "Uh . . . yes, sir. Luke is out front. Why don't we go tell him the good news?"

"You go ahead, girl. I need to round up my men first. I'll be right along." Captain Chandler placed his hat back on his head and moved away through the crowd.

"Come on, Abby," Pastor Achilles said, leading

her by the arm from the smoky tavern. "This is no place for an innocent like yourself."

When they reached the wooden boardwalk, Luke rose. "Abby, what's wrong? You're as white as a ghost."

"Nothing." She swallowed and glanced nervously out to sea.

A few seconds later, the captain joined them, and they made their introductions as they began walking to the harbor.

"Horatio, are you dropping off stock in Honolulu, then heading to China as usual?" the pastor asked.

"Yes. We've still got some goods from California to unload in Honolulu, but we've a full load of sandalwood for the Chinese. They love the scent. I can sell every last board there for a grand profit." His boots sounded loudly on the harbor's wooden dock.

"Here we are, children, at the captain's skiff," Pastor Achilles said, indicating the sixteen-foot boat tied to the dock. He shook hands with Abby and Luke. "Godspeed," he said enthusiastically. "Horatio, thank you." He gripped the captain's hand warmly. "Give even a cup of cold water in His name, and you'll receive your reward in heaven."

Captain Chandler looked momentarily stricken. "To be reunited is all I ask," he murmured. Then the captain turned to greet his two men, who waited in the skiff, and made introductions. "Mr. Job, here, is my first mate." He inclined his head toward a small, white-haired man in the sailor's typical uniform of duck cloth. "If you need anything, speak to him."

The captain picked Abby up by the waist and lowered her to Job. "This is Abigail and her friend Luke."

Mr. Job caught and steadied her in the bottom of the tipsy skiff. "There ye go, girl. Are ye joinin' us on our sail now?"

Captain Chandler stepped down into the skiff, causing it to rock violently. "Aye, she and the boy were lost in their own ship's dinghy. They'll be catching a ride with us to Oahu, where the child's parents are." He took a seat at the bow of the boat.

Job spoke to Luke. "Young man," he directed, "untie the line and toss it in, and yerself, too, if ye be wantin' to tag along."

Luke bent to the task by the light of a full moon. He tossed the line to Job and leapt into the back of the skiff. "How long until we leave?" he asked.

The captain took out his pocket watch and consulted it. "In less than three hours, lad."

As Mr. Job bent to the oars, Abby sat rigidly on the wooden bench, listening to the soft sound of oars dipping into the black sea. She was doubly glad to be leaving Lahaina and the dark-haired beast who'd come toward her. Trying to shake the mood, Abby searched the bay. "Is that your ship, Captain?"

She pointed to a three-masted barkentine that lay silver in the moonlight.

"Aye, that's her. A finer woman I've never known." The captain turned to wink at Abby.

Abby gave the captain a weak smile. It faded as her mind pored over the evening's events. Abby was troubled. By all accounts, things now *looked* right. They were finally on their way to Ma and Pa and a joyful reunion. She should be glad.

But she was growing more unsettled, as if trouble lay brewing secretly in the dark. . . . as if she were swimming in a black sea, and underneath lurked unseen sharks.

Chapter Thirteen

A sailor let down a rope ladder as the skiff came alongside the barkentine in choppy waves. It was hard to stand and move toward the ladder, and it was even harder for Abby to climb up the rope as the sea heaved. Luke had gone up first, and he leaned down to grab Abby's hand.

"Here now," said Mr. Job, as soon as he'd climbed aboard, "whyn't ye two sit at the bow and bide yer time. We'll be readyin' the ship, and we need ye outa harm's way."

Abby and Luke settled themselves against the bulkhead near the bow, watching the ship's skiff make a trip back to the dock, collecting sailors. From the bay, Lahaina looked peaceful with its twinkling lights reflecting on the water, but they could still hear the rowdy sounds of wild sailors from shore.

"It's much nicer traveling out in the open than under a tarp," Luke said quietly. Abby only nodded. She had grown tired from their long, long day.

Leaning against the bulkhead and against each other, with the sea rocking gently, the two drifted off to sleep.

Abby kicked out violently. The shark had passed just out of reach, its beady black eyes targeting her eerily, its jaws opening and closing as if it were tasting her scent. Then she couldn't see it, didn't know where it was until its rough skin scraped her bare leg as it came in to take a bite. . . .

"Ahh!" She thrashed as the sandpaper-rough skin grazed her leg again.

"Abby!" Luke shook her awake, but the realization that she had only been dreaming came slowly. She noticed the ship rocking, saw distant stars behind Luke's head, and heard the rigging squeal as sailors pulled lines through the tackle. She rubbed the sleep from her eyes and looked east. Lahaina was no longer there!

"Luke, we're moving." He grinned at her and pointed above them. Sure enough, the sails were full, pale in the moonlight.

"I woke as we got under way," he said, "but I thought I'd let you sleep. Only you must've been having a nightmare. Were you dreaming about Aunt Dagmar?" His teeth shone like white pearls.

"Nothing like that," Abby answered. But suddenly some sandpaper brushed her leg, making her jump.

Luke reached across her and scooted the rough hemp rope off to the side. Abby sighed as she realized that was what had made her dream of shark skin scratching her!

"I guess all's well that ends well," she said. Her worries had been silly. Soon she'd arrive on Oahu and would see Ma, Pa, and Sarah. *God, I'm so grateful. . . .*

The sounds of men at work on the ship and the slap of water against the hull eased Abby from the dread of her dream as she smoothed her dress and began braiding her hair to keep it from flying in her face.

Captain Chandler's voice boomed out above everything else. "Hoist the jib, Mr. Jackal."

"Aye, Cap'n," came the reply.

Abby's fingers stopped. She gaped in stunned silence.

Luke smoothed a stray hair off her face, concern etched across his features. "What is it, Ab?"

"That voice—" she whispered, "it's the sailor from town."

Luke noticed the sailor who'd answered the captain. He was heading their way!

The muscular man bent to release the jib line from its cleat. For a moment Luke could not tell if it was Jackal or not. But when he straightened, there was no mistaking the black beard and ruthless face that greeted him. "Out of me way, boy!" he shouted as he heaved the line, stretching the sail taut.

Luke watched as Abby rose quickly. When Jackal tied off the line, he began winding the remainder of it into a coil. That's when he spotted Abby.

His mouth opened as his eyebrows drew together in a menacing line. "What?" he shouted angrily. "The devil's teeth! What's a girl doin' onboard?"

Abby's heart thudded with fear, but she planted her feet firmly on the moving deck and took a deep breath. "We're traveling to Oahu with Captain Chandler," she said. She was mortified to hear her voice quiver.

"That's right," Captain Chandler said, coming up behind Jackal. "Do you have a problem with my decision, sailor?"

Jackal pierced Abby with a look of hatred. "Everyone knows a girl's bad luck onboard ship! There's a reason sailors don't like women aboard."

The captain put an arm around Abby's shoulder. "She is my guest and will be treated as one. Do I make myself clear, Mr. Jackal?" The threat of discipline was plain in his voice.

"Aye, ye have." Jackal scowled at Abby before he threw down the coil of rope at her feet and stomped off. "Jinxed the ship, ye have," he said under his breath. Abby could hear murmurs of disapproval coming from the men nearby. Were they agreeing with Jackal or disgusted with his behavior?

"Abby, you and Luke join me for a late supper

before bed. Come with me to my cabin," the captain said. He led the way down the hatch belowdecks, giving an order to the cook in the galley to serve them in his room. As they headed toward the aft of the ship, they ran into two sailors whispering in the hall. The men grew silent as the captain neared. Abby's sense of apprehension increased.

When they reached his cabin, Captain Chandler pulled out a chair for Abby to sit on at the small dining table. She was grateful to be away from the prying eyes of sailors. Taking in her surroundings, she was amazed at how beautiful the captain's cabin was. A row of broad windows at the back of the ship overlooked the sea, and she could see stars through them.

The captain's bunk was built into the wall but was covered with a thick quilt in the wedding-ring pattern. Above his bunk hung two paintings: one of a beautiful lady with dark eyes and hair, the other of a young boy in a sailor suit with a wide collar and breeches. When he saw Abby staring at them, Captain Chandler explained. "That is my wife, Isobel, and our son, David. He went to sea with me, but we lost him last year."

A quietness descended over the cabin. Luke cleared his throat, his face almost as stricken as the captain's. "I'm sorry for your loss, sir."

"Luke lost his family, too, Captain Chandler, to cholera," Abby explained.

"My sympathies, son." The captain rose and paced. "To lose your loved ones is a great cross to bear." He cleared his throat as if trying to swallow some emotion. "When I saw you two in Lahaina, I knew I had to help you get home. There could be no greater gift I could give than to return a child, once thought dead, to a grieving parent."

He paused, then resumed his pacing with his hands behind his back. "I'm sorry for the words of Mr. Jackal. He's given me worries ever since I signed him on in Brazil last year, to replace my son. We were shorthanded, and I had to take on whomever I could. I admit I have not attended to the men this year as I normally do. My loss and my worry about Isobel have occupied me. But now I sense a growing darkness. . . ." The captain stopped, as if he thought better of divulging any more. "At any rate, I plan to remedy the situation soon."

Just then the cook entered, bearing a silver tray of dishes. Abby and Luke smelled the delicious food and lost no time in joining the captain in dinner. Roast pig, potatoes, sliced fruit, and sweet bread made up the meal. After a delightful feast, the captain had his coffee and told tales of his travels along the coast of South America. In the midst of it, the cook came in to clear the plates, stacking them back on the silver tray, and left the cabin. After the door shut, however, a loud clattering in the hallway brought Captain Chandler to his feet.

He strode to his door and peered into the dim

hallway. Then as Abby and Luke watched, the captain backed up with his hands above his head, rage spreading over his face.

"Mr. Jackal, what is this?"

Jackal erupted in a laugh that sent chills down Abby's back. He stalked into the cabin, waving a pistol at the captain's heart. "Ye're not so high and mighty now, are ye, Cap'n?" When he laughed again, his rotting teeth and black, beady eyes reminded Abby of the shark in her nightmare, watching her with icy malice.

"Get up, ye useless brats. Ye can join yer cap'n on deck for a little announcement I'm goin' to make." He aimed the pistol at Abby and Luke briefly, then pointed it back at the captain. They filed out and marched up the hatch to the deck.

When they got there, the sailors on deck joined them. "Here now, what's goin' on with ye?" Mr. Job asked, clearly distressed.

"If'n ye want to bellyache with the cap'n, ye can join him, Mr. Job. There's plenty of room at the bottom of the sea for ye, too!"

Then Jackal threw back his head and roared, his black beard piercing the sky. Six sailors joined in. Abby could see they were already in on his devious plans.

"We be takin' yer ship, Cap'n, for we've plans of our own. First, we be off to China to sell the booty. Then we'll return here for buried treasure!" There were gasps from the other fourteen men who hadn't known about the mutiny. "Anyone who doesn't join us can gladly go with the cap'n to the bottom of the sea. All right, who's with us?" he shouted, waving the pistol.

Mr. Job stepped forward. He stood only as tall as Jackal's shoulder, but he drew himself up to his full height, his white hair glinting in the moonlight. "How do we know ye have a treasure?" he asked.

"Take this, Spandler," Jackal said, as he handed the pistol over to a sailor with a silver earring. Then he reached inside his shirt and brought out the rolled-up scroll of leather. "Here it is, lads—the map to make ye rich!"

Shouts went up from the six crewmen who were part of the mutiny. The others stared, some confused and some beginning to rub their hands in glee at the thought of easy treasure. Mr. Job looked stricken, but he kept his mouth shut in a tight line. *They are drunk with greed!* Abby thought in horror. *Oh, poor Captain Chandler.*

Jackal stuffed the map back in his shirt. "Then it's decided. Ye're outvoted, Cap'n, though we hold ye no ill will." Abby gasped, covering her mouth with a shaking hand. If the captain was made to walk the plank, she and Luke would be left alone with this madman!

Jackal focused his attention on her, tugging her braid so hard she cried out in pain. "Don't worry, Little Shark Bait, the cap'n won't leave ye. Ye'll be joinin' him at the bottom of the sea!" Abby felt like a fist had slammed into her stomach; she couldn't catch her breath.

"Boy," Jackal said, addressing Luke, "if'n ye want to live, ye can join us men and learn ye a trade that will make ye rich."

Luke put his fists in front of Jackal's face. "Why don't you pick on someone your own size, you hairy pirate!" Jackal sobered, then slammed a fist into Luke's mouth, sending him sprawling across the teak deck.

"Luke!" Abby ran to him, cradling his unconscious head in her lap. Blood oozed from his cut lip. Shaking with rage, she glared up at Jackal. "You, you . . . shark . . . you . . . varmint! You beast!"

"Git 'em all overboard!" Jackal yelled angrily. "The girl's a jinx to our plans." Several sailors began to move toward her. When one grabbed her roughly by the arms, tearing her away from Luke, Abby screamed in terror.

Luke came to then, but he couldn't move right away. Dragged to the railing, Abby peered over and realized her worst nightmare was coming true. In another second, she would be swimming in the sea with the sharks—sharks that came from below with sandpaper skin and razor-sharp teeth.

Chapter Fourteen

"Hold up!" yelled Mr. Job. "What's the sense in feedin' the fishes when we could sell the girl, the boy, and the captain for good money in China? Ye know how they love to buy white slaves there!"

For a moment no one spoke, then most of the sailors nodded, murmuring agreement. Mr. Job seemed to sense their approval and spoke quickly. "Why should we be lettin' superstition cloud our judgment, boys? Why should we be passin' up easy gold, especially when they can serve us the whole way there?"

Jackal rubbed his dirty beard in thought and glanced around at the crew. Abby sensed the crew didn't want to kill Captain Chandler—they only wanted to get rich. Most agreed with Mr. Job. Abby could see Jackal didn't want to push the crew too far.

"Good thinkin', Job. Aye, it makes more sense, it does. With a fine crew like this, what bad luck have we to fear? Let it be done. They kin serve us like slaves. . . ." His voice boomed out, "Just for practice, lock 'em up below!"

Then his face grew serious. "Turner, git the firearms from the cap'n's cabin and bring 'em to me. Then break out the rum. A double ration for each man to start the journey right!"

More loud shouts of approval went up into the night as Mr. Job herded the captain and kids belowdecks. Abby's blood roared in her ears. Luke had been struck by that evil man, that Judas who betrayed the captain. They had barely escaped death, she realized, as she supported Luke under his arm on their way to the cabin. She was trembling in the emotional aftermath.

When they reached the captain's cabin, Turner took the key from the captain and unlocked the firearm cabinet. He loaded twelve muskets into the arms of two other men and took four himself. Then he tossed the room key to Job. "Lock 'em in," he said as they exited.

Job spoke in a whisper. "Cap'n, I can't be standin' against the whole crew, but I'll do what I can for ye."

Captain Chandler put his hand on Mr. Job's forearm. "I'm grateful to you for our lives, Mr. Job. If it weren't for you . . ." The captain shook his head in apparent anguish. "Mr. Job, I ask one more favor."

"Aye, sir, anythin' I can do."

"At the end of each day, after the children have worked, see if you can't convince Jackal to let them sleep in whatever cabin or hole you put me. We can be a support to each other, and . . . I don't want them harmed by drunken sailors." The captain's eyes pierced Mr. Job.

"Aye, sir, I takes yer point. I'll do what I can."

"If you do that, Mr. Job, I shall not forget you."

It seemed to Abby that an unspoken agreement had passed between the two men. For the first time that night, a spark of hope ignited inside her.

In the face of such evil, friendship could make all the difference. As Mr. Job shut the door and locked it, she was comforted. At least she was nowhere near Jackal, a man whose mother, she decided, had named him well. Jackals, Abby knew, were wild dogs that hunted their prey at night.

Captain Chandler swept the beautiful quilt off his bed and laid it on the floor. "This will do as a bed for tonight, Abby," he said. "Luke, you can sleep in that corner over there."

"Thank you, sir," Luke said, settling down with another blanket.

Abby took the tea towel over to the water pitcher and wet one end. "Here, Luke. Set this against your swollen lip," she offered, holding it against his lip. Luke winced, then smiled ruefully at her.

"You're a brave lad," the captain said. "You remind me of David, my son." Once again he began to pace, hands behind his back. "I swear," he said, stopping and looking intently at them, "with God's help, I will get us off this ship and away from Jackal.

That animal has infected my whole crew with a lust for gold! But for now, we've got to get some rest so we can face whatever tomorrow brings."

The captain knelt beside his bunk, and the children followed his lead. "Heavenly Father," he began, "be with us now in our hour of need. Let no harm come to us. Give Your angels charge concerning us, to guard us in all our ways. And turn the hearts of my crew back to what is right and good and true." The captain paused and sighed. "Lord, bless Isobel with Your comfort while we are apart. And uphold Abby's parents with Your strength until she can be reunited with them. Strengthen Luke and bless him for his courage. In Jesus' name I pray. Amen."

Captain Chandler rose and trimmed the oil lamp, and the cabin was encased in darkness. Abby gazed out the large window in search of starlight. Somehow it comforted her to see the ancient stars shining still, like points of hope. The very same stars Ma might be watching at this moment. She settled herself on the quilt.

Oh, Pa, she thought, *we're in such a fix . . . and you can't help me.* Those words struck Abby with immediate clarity. When they were lost in the jollyboat, God had stilled the storm to a whisper. He could help them now, too!

Oh, God, I don't know how we could end up in such a mess. This is worse than being lost at sea! But

You rescued us then. Please rescue us now. Don't let Luke and me be sold into slavery!

She was glad no one could see the tears sliding down her cheeks. But then, there came a Presence, a Peace, that spoke in her unsettled mind.

BE STRONG AND BRAVE, FOR I AM WITH YOU. I HAVE NOT LEFT YOU AS ORPHANS. I AM WITH YOU—TO PROTECT AND WATCH OVER YOU, LIKE THE ANCIENT STARS.

But, how could You let us fall into the hands of Jackal? He's so evil!

DO NOT BE AFRAID. I AM WITH YOU. AND I KNOW THE PLANS I HAVE FOR YOU, TO GIVE YOU A FUTURE AND A HOPE.

His Presence surrounded her, and she believed— not because Ma and Pa did, but because He was real. For the first time in her life, Abby realized how much she loved Him. Tears of gratitude flooded her eyes. *He cares for me!*

She'd heard His voice, and it made all the difference. *I guess that's faith—when you believe what He says.* As she closed her eyes, a peaceful sleep found her.

The sound of a key in the lock entered her consciousness. The door swung open, revealing Mr. Job with a lantern at the same moment as four bells struck, signaling the third half-hour of morning watch. "It's 5:30, children," Mr. Job said softly. "Time to rise."

The captain, who had also slept in his clothes and was wide awake, leaned over and gently shook Abby. "Wake up, child, and pray the Lord shields you today."

Abby leapt to her feet. Out the window she could see the barest hint of light on the eastern horizon.

Luke rose, too, his lip still swollen and now black and blue. "Time for breakfast?" he asked Mr. Job.

"Time to swab the deck, boy. If yer lucky, the devil hisself will let ye eat some victuals."

As Mr. Job herded all but the captain from the cabin, Captain Chandler stopped him. "Mr. Job, wait a minute." He placed a hand on Abby's shoulder and one on Luke's while he uttered a short prayer. "Oh merciful Lord, be with Your children this day, and protect them from evil."

Mr. Job frowned. "Hurry now. Jackal's sleepin' off his rum, but he left me instructions."

"Did you convince him to let the children stay with me?" the captain asked.

Mr. Job stopped the swinging lantern, casting an eerie light on his face. "Aye, but who knows how long it'll last? For tonight ye can stay in yer cabin. The men took a vote on account of ye always treatin' them good." In the hallway, Abby watched him set down the lantern and relock the door.

Abby prayed silently for their protection. *Oh, Lord, don't let us be sold in slavery! Ma and Pa will never see me again.* She thought about what it would be like to never see them again, to not see little Sarah grow up. She held back a gasp. *But this is what Luke is dealing with,* she realized. *He'll never see his ma and pa again on earth. . . . Oh God, please don't let that happen to me. Give us back our lives!*

There was no answering voice. But as Abby climbed topside, the sun's rays broke over the distant horizon, and she remembered God's words, harkening back thousands of years to the days of the Old Testament: *I AM WITH YOU AND WILL WATCH OVER YOU WHEREVER YOU GO.* And she was glad, very glad, that her mother had read out loud from the Bible each day.

Sunrise came and went, and still Abby and Luke worked without food. It had been at least three hours since they'd risen, she guessed. Her stomach growled loudly. They had swabbed the whole deck and polished the brass. They had tarred the shrouds within reach, and Luke had climbed the ratlines to do the higher rigging. Now she sat wearily on the bulkhead, her legs shaking with fatigue. She was afraid to rest, but she had to.

When footsteps sounded behind her, Abby jumped up. But it was Mr. Job.

"Abby, ye and Luke can go grab a morsel of food. Ye best go quick, before anyone gives ye more work to do." He didn't have to tell Luke, who had heard and was already climbing down the shrouds hand over hand like a monkey.

His bare feet hit the deck. "Come on, Ab. You need a break, and my stomach's as empty as a bear's on the first day of spring."

They made their way to the galley, where the cook set down two bowls of cold, congealed oatmeal on a wooden table built into the wall. A whale-oil lamp hung from the low ceiling, swaying slightly with the roll and pitch of the ship. Set into the wall was a caddy holding a saltshaker and a large wooden peppershaker, the tallest spice grinder Abby had ever seen. Perhaps it was from a faraway land, like India, from which so many spices came. Apparently it was there for the sailors' evening meals. But this morning's meal was cereal, and Abby could see that some kind of bug had been cooked in with the mush.

She looked longingly at the wooden bowl of bananas and papayas on the table. Cautiously she took a papaya and held it close to her nose, breathing in its ripe scent. How she wanted to take a succulent bite, but she was afraid to ask permission from the cook—maybe he was a friend of Jackal's.

"Luke," Abby mouthed quietly, "there are bugs in this mush!"

"You've got to eat, Ab. No telling when we'll get a chance to escape. But you're gonna need all your strength when the time comes."

Too tired to talk anymore, the kids ate around the bugs and then laid their heads on the table to rest. Within minutes, the ship's bells struck. Abby raised her head. "Luke, it's only ten in the morning, and I'm worn out already."

Luke scrubbed his face tiredly. "Go slow, Ab. Conserve your strength."

"I'll try," she said, biting her lower lip. *Oh, how could we have gotten into this horrible jam?* They had escaped drowning in a storm on the high seas, only to be caught in the midst of a mutiny—and were now on their way to becoming slaves in China!

The cook evaluated them with narrowed eyes. "What are you two talkin' about?" he asked, his voice a low growl.

Luke sat up straight. "Nothing, sir."

The cook wiped greasy hands on his filthy apron and picked up two long knives. He eyed them as he began slicing the knives back and forth on each other to sharpen them. He walked toward Abby, grating the knives back and forth, back and forth, their sharp edges glinting in the lamplight.

Suddenly he raised one high above them. Abby's eyes widened as the knife came down like a guillotine and sliced through the papaya with a loud whomp, sending the papaya halves sailing across the table. Black shiny seeds spilled onto the wooden tabletop. The cook laughed at Abby's shock as he tugged the butcher knife free of the wood.

"Have some papaya," he said, his dark eyes glinting at her. "It keeps scurvy away." He walked back to his bubbling pot and began chopping onions for stew.

Abby wore a shocked expression. Luke's eyebrows arched as he leaned forward. "He and Aunt Dagmar would make a perfect couple." She grinned.

Luke rose with their dishes, depositing them next to the wash pot. "Thanks for the meal," he said. "We'll finish our fruit topside." The two left the galley quickly and breathed deeply when they emerged into the fresh air and sunshine.

For a few minutes they were kids again, spitting papaya seeds into the waves.

"Jackal wants the railin' polished next," Mr. Job said, coming up behind them. "Abby, when that's done, ye're to deliver the cap'n's meal to him. I'll open the locked door for ye when it's time."

"Yes, sir." As she and Luke picked up rags to begin their next job, her heart brightened at the thought of seeing Captain Chandler so soon.

Perhaps he's thought of a plan to set us free!

Chapter Fifteen

When Mr. Job unlocked the door to the captain's cabin, Abby saw the captain standing with head bowed before the great picture windows. "We've come with your lunch, sir," she said, hoping to rouse him from what appeared to be a sad mood.

He moved toward them, his shiny brass buttons still reflecting the light that streamed through the stern of the ship, but his eyes were dull. *The captain needs cheering up,* Abby thought. *And why shouldn't he? His own men have betrayed him for gold . . . just like Judas betrayed Jesus for thirty pieces of silver. Oh, the poor man!*

"Cook sent ye some fresh fruit, Cap'n, along with stew and bread." Mr. Job seemed uncomfortable at the sight of Captain Chandler's sad face. He headed toward the door.

"Thank you, Mr. Job. Will the ship be docking in Honolulu tonight?"

Mr. Job grimaced. "No, sir. Jackal said the ship will sell all she's carryin' in China."

"I suppose that includes the children and me?"

Mr. Job placed a hand on the doorknob, his eyes on the floor. He spoke in a bare whisper. "Aye, sir, he's stickin' to his plans. If ye give me yer word, sir, as a gentleman, I'll be leavin' the door unlocked for a bit so ye and the girl can visit." Abby realized it was a gift, a way to try to soften the blow. He left the room and closed the door, but there was no sound of the lock clicking.

"He feels bad about this, Captain."

"You're right, Abby. Mr. Job has served me well for seven years." He paused, running his hand through his thick hair. "I just can't believe it's come to this. The men should be horsewhipped . . . or hung," he growled.

Abby set the tray down at his dining table. "Maybe you should eat something, Captain."

He nodded briefly. "Sit with me."

Abby saluted with a smile, and the captain laughed out loud. "There," he said, "you've broken my bad mood." He began to eat with enthusiasm.

"Captain, have you figured out a way to get us freed?"

He sighed and set down his bread. "I've prayed all morning, child. But as yet, I can't see how we can overpower so many men . . . or even a few to win our way to the guns. Worse than that, I'm not sure where the powder and shot is being kept, even if we could get the guns."

Abby sat facing the great window, tugging at her

lower lip in thought. "What if we don't need the guns? What if we just slip away without anyone seeing us?"

"You mean jump overboard in the midst of the sea?"

"No. . . . Luke and I were set adrift in a skiff—but we made it to land. What if we lowered the skiff and sailed away from the ship?"

The captain's brown eyes bored into hers. "You mean sneak away when no one is looking?" he asked.

"Exactly! Why, we can do it tonight."

The captain stroked his chin. He spoke more to himself than to her. "We'd certainly have to do it tonight. We'll be passing Oahu around midnight; after that it's a long way to land again."

"Then tonight it is!" Abby jumped up and moved toward the window. "Do these open, Captain?"

The captain was deep in thought. "What?"

"These windows, do they open?"

"Only one, girl. The small one on the side, to let in a breeze. But why do you ask?"

Abby fumbled with the latch. "We'll need a way to get topside tonight, so you and Luke can lower the skiff."

Suddenly the door opened. Abby stood still as a mouse, her hand frozen on the latch.

"What are you doing?" Luke asked, as he entered the cabin.

"Luke, you scared the skin off me!" Abby went back to work at the latch.

"Captain," Luke asked, "what's Abby up to?" He came up behind her to inspect the window.

The captain joined them. "This blue-eyed beauty has come up with a plan, boy—a plan to set us free!" Both children stared at him as he deftly lifted the latch and the window swung open. The cool Hawaiian trade winds blew through, bringing the scent of the sea and freedom to Abby.

Grinning, Abby poked Luke in the stomach. "It's going to work, Luke. I just know it."

"Abigail," the captain said, "if your hopefulness was a cold, I'd be sneezing. Who knows, but with the help of the Almighty, it just might work." He tousled Abby's thick hair and hugged her close. "Thank you, child," he murmured.

Turning to Luke, he gave orders. "The two of you get in here tonight as soon as you can. As far as I can tell, we should be passing the island around midnight. But if you can keep your ears open for any talk among the men, that would help. We need information."

Luke saluted with mischief. "Aye, aye, sir. We'll be your eyes and ears topside."

"You'll make a dandy sailor someday, Luke. But for now, you'd best be on your way. I don't want anyone to know we're in here planning."

"Back to the slave galley," Abby joked.

As they headed toward the door, the captain

pierced them with a serious look. "A word of warning: Stay away from Jackal."

The smile died on Abby's lips. It was good advice, advice she'd like to heed. But how did one stay clear of a brute while captive on the beast's own floating kingdom?

The day dragged on. The ship's bell and wheel were cleaned. The sextant and other brass instruments were polished. Potatoes were peeled for the evening dinner. And the deck was scrubbed again at dusk. Finally Luke and Abby were sent to the captain's cabin with dry bread and a watery potato soup.

The captain bowed his head to thank God in spite of the unappetizing meal. After supper, he ordered Abby to the bunk to rest. "You'll need your strength tonight, so try to get some sleep."

It seemed she had only laid her head down a minute when the door swung open and Spandler, Jackal's right-hand man, stood over her, reeking of rum and sweat. "Wake up, girl. The cap'n wants ye and yer friend back at work." His spittle flew at her when he spoke. She sat up and backed away on the bunk. "Ye're to serve 'im in the galley tonight."

He glowered at her in the dim lantern light and then stalked out. Luke jumped up from his spot on the window seat, where he'd been talking with the captain. His fists were clenched at his sides. "It's all right, Abby. I'll be with you."

The captain gripped a chair, his knuckles white. As he stared out the window, she saw that he, too, was angry—but not at her.

Abby peered out the window, but she wasn't looking at the stars in the twilight. She was watching the reflection in the glass of a young girl, her long curls tucked into a single braid with her usual stray strands of ringlets hanging about her face. Her blue dress, which had fit her perfectly at the start of their journey from California, hung loosely about her waist. *I'm at my fighting weight,* Abby thought, surprising herself with an unexpected spunk. *I have God on my side, and He's brought me through this far.* She watched as the girl in the glass straightened. Her shoulders went back and her chin went up.

"Don't be overcome by evil, but overcome evil with good," Abby said. Captain Chandler jumped at her words. As she gazed at his reflection in the glass, she could see that his look of anger had disappeared, and in its place was something akin to admiration.

"Luke," he said, facing them both, "Abby's right. You two work hard and trust in God. Jackal surely won't keep you all night, so as soon as you get back, we'll make good our escape."

Luke scowled. "How can you and Abby trust in

something unseen when we're dealing with that
devil?"

The captain put a calloused hand on Luke's
shoulder. "When you're dealing with the devil, boy,
God is all you can trust in."

Abby retraced her steps to the bunk and retrieved
her high-button boots. Lacing them up, she glanced
over at Luke. "Let's go."

Abby and Luke headed toward the galley, where
Jackal expected them to serve his dinner. But as
they neared it, they could hear singing   wild,
drunken sounds.

Fifteen men on a dead man's ship!
Yo, ho, ho, and a bottle of rum!

Abby swallowed hard. She'd never heard men
behave like this before— not until they'd passed
through Lahaina. Her mind flooded with the image
of Jackal flying out of the grogshop and fisting the
sailor in the street. She could see his biceps bulging
in the tight shirt, smell his sweat, and feel her own
fear again as she recalled his words, "That'll help
ye remember me in the mornin'!" Then that
sickening thud as his boot hit the fallen man's
stomach.

Abby and Luke stopped close to the galley and

heard Jackal's ruthless voice. "Aye, and we'll sell six of the men in China, too. That way there'll be less men to share the plunder with!"

Luke drew in a quick breath, but Abby was not surprised Jackal was willing to cheat his own men, for he had no scruples, no morals. The devil was the father of lies, and Jackal was his son. *I don't want to face him, Father. I'm afraid.*

DO NOT BE AFRAID. I AM WITH YOU, AND I WILL WATCH OVER YOU WHEREVER YOU GO.

Even in the galley?

IF YOU GO TO THE DEPTHS OF THE SEA, I AM THERE.

But with such evil men?

ESPECIALLY AS YOU FACE DARKNESS—FOR IT IS AS LIGHT TO ME.

Abby lifted her head. She was afraid, but she also trusted God. She threw her braid over her shoulder and took a deep breath. As she stepped into the glow of the galley's lantern light, a peace filled her.

The talking abruptly stopped.

Jackal scrutinized her, his eyes like shiny black marbles rimmed in red. Two other men sat at the table with him—Spandler and the cook. They grinned at the kids, but not in a friendly way.

"Girl," Jackal bellowed, "bring me dinner!"

Abby could see he was already deep in his cups— sloppy drunk. The whole galley smelled of rum and unwashed bodies.

"You, boy," Spandler directed, "come with me

and Cookie to the bilge. We've got to haul supplies up."

Abby caught Luke's glance of concern for her. But there was no use arguing, she knew. It was best to get the work done and get back to the captain. With God's help they'd soon be gone. She nodded at Luke as he and the two men left for the lower deck.

Abby obediently went to the counter, where she ladled soup from a large pot into a bowl. Carefully she set it before Jackal. He glared at her. "Now git some bread!"

When she returned with a large hunk, he gestured at the bench. "Sit down."

Abby did but wondered what he wanted. "I don't like ye," Jackal began, slurring slightly. "Girls don't belong onboard ship. Where'd ye come from, anyway?"

"Luke and I went overboard in a storm. We came ashore a few miles west of Lahaina." It took a moment for her story to register with him, but finally he threw back his head and cackled.

"Ye fell out of a ship only to get caught in the middle of a mutiny? I told ye—girls shouldn't sail!" He laughed uproariously, food splashing out of his mouth. "How'd ye like the idea of goin' sightseein' in China?"

Abby wondered why he was asking her these questions. She did not trust him or his motives. "God is with me!" she blurted out.

141

Jackal leapt from his seat, spilling the soup, and reached across the table for her wrist. "Don't talk to me about God!" he spat out. "Me mother believed in Him, but she went to her grave early. There *is* no God!"

Abby winced as his meaty fist closed around her wrist and pinched her hard. She stared into his bloodshot eyes until he lowered his gaze. "Mr. Jackal, I'm sorry about your loss. I can't explain all the heartache that happens, but I know God cares."

Jackal flushed as he caught her eye. For a brief moment Abby thought she'd made a connection with him. But then his eyes hardened, and he flung her wrist back at her. "Ye're dangerous. Just like the cap'n. Tonight I'm makin' some changes. Soon as Spandler gets back, I'll have 'im move yer dear cap'n to the bilge." He got up and moved around the table toward her then. "In the meantime, ye'll spend yer nights tied up here. And yer little friend will be tied up topside."

Abby's heart did a double jump. If Jackal gave those orders, they'd never get a chance to escape! They'd be sold in China, and she'd never see Ma, Pa, or Sarah again!

Jackal staggered over to the corner of the galley and retrieved a coil of rope hanging on the wall. As he neared her, Abby panicked. She had to do something. When he bent to wrap the rope around the center leg of the table, Abby didn't even think. She just reached for the giant peppershaker and raised it above her head.

Whack! The cracking sound was loud in her ears as the peppershaker connected with Jackal's skull. The blow momentarily stunned him. He fell face down onto the tabletop amid a pile of black peppercorns, then careened onto the table bench.

Abby's eyes almost bulged out of her head. She knew if he came to she would be instant shark bait!

I've got to get out of here! She fled toward the doorway but stopped short with a terrifying thought: *What if I've killed him?* She gulped and turned slowly around. She just had to know if he was breathing. Fear made her heart pound furiously as she moved back toward the table. There was no sign of life; only the back of his head and neck showed from where she stood. She would have to get closer.

Abby moved around the end of the table and stopped within two feet of him, but she still couldn't see. She bent down on one knee, staring intently at his chest. It was hidden beneath the table. But it was no good. There wasn't enough light to see whether or not he was breathing. She did not dare touch him to find out.

Abby dragged a chair over to the lantern, then climbed up to lift it from its hook on the ceiling. Hurrying back to Jackal, she set the lantern under the table, where the light could shine on his belly and chest. She kneeled down and peered up under the table.

He's breathing! Relieved, Abby reached for the lantern. But just as she was about to flee, Abby noticed something sticking out of the front of Jackal's shirt—a bit of leather. *The treasure map!*

Abby's pounding heart did a triple-time beat. She could scarcely breathe. *Should I take it?* Her hand began to reach out, almost of its own accord, and her knees inched over to within a foot of him. She touched the edge of the leather scroll, held her breath, and began to tug gently. It wouldn't budge. She'd have to move his arm to free it.

As she inched closer, her hair brushed against Jackal's knees. She gingerly lifted his arm and slid the map out with shaking fingers. Just as she turned to scramble away, he groaned. She didn't wait to see if he would awaken. Abby raced for the doorway, tucking the treasure map down her front-buttoned dress.

She ran all the way to Captain Chandler's cabin and threw open the door. Gasping for breath, she slammed the door shut.

Captain Chandler jumped up and came over, looking deep into her eyes. Luke joined them. "Abby, are you all right?" She could see concern on both of their faces.

"Yes, I'm all right, but now's a good time to take leave of Jackal's company, if you get my meaning."

Her flushed face and dilated eyes were all the

explanation Captain Chandler needed. "It's almost time by my reckoning, anyway. Luke, let's get the window open and climb up." The two hurried to the window and unlatched it. From inside the window seat Captain Chandler produced a coil of thick hemp rope. On one end a loop was tied. "Abby, you're to jump to us when we give the signal. Do you understand, girl?"

"Yes!" With or without a signal, she was more than ready to leave the ship! If Jackal woke up, or if Spandler discovered he wasn't actually asleep . . .

Captain Chandler climbed out first and balanced cautiously on the windowsill. Luke tied one end of the rope to the latch on the window seat, while the captain took the other end with him. Gripping the top of the window with his left hand, he swung the rope in a circle the way Abby had seen caballeros throw lariats around cattle in California. But she couldn't see where the looped end of the rope had landed. He tried several times before it apparently hit its mark on the deck above, for the captain gripped the rope with both hands and pulled himself up hand over hand. Luke followed.

Alone in the cabin, Abby could feel her legs begin to tremble. She leaned out the window and inhaled the salty sea air. *Take deep breaths,* she told herself. *It will be over soon.*

She sucked in the cool trade winds, but she couldn't shake the feeling of impending doom.

Chapter Sixteen

Luke and Captain Chandler had been gone four or
five minutes when Abby heard a thump on the ceiling above her. *Oh, please don't let them get caught!*
In her mind's eye, she could see the mutineers
discovering them and throwing them overboard.
The last thing she wanted was to be stuck onboard
without Luke.

Abby gripped the windowsill and leaned out. She
hoped for a glimpse of them up above or on their
way back down. Just as she retreated back, something large was lowered in the spot where she'd
been. *The skiff!* Abby wanted to reach out and grab
it, get into it, and escape. *Anywhere is safer than
here.* But the boat sailed by her too quickly.

She watched as the skiff lowered toward the
water. When it hit, the boat made a slight splash.

Abby held her breath. *Has someone heard it?*
Tense moments passed. When no cry of alarm was
raised, she sighed with relief.

The boat trailed behind the ship, tethered by the

rope that had lowered it. Abby noted in dismay that it didn't stay right behind the ship but arched away from the ship.

"I hope no one on watch sees it!" she said aloud. Then Abby silently urged Luke and the captain, *Hurry, hurry! Come down!*

She peered out the window into the dark and was shocked to see Luke's tan shirt gliding through the air. He was sailing down the rope that was suspended between the ship and skiff. When he got to the small boat, Luke pulled himself aboard. Seconds later, Abby saw a triangle of white gliding through the air. It was the captain's cravat!

She was alone on the ship with Jackal, and the skiff had disappeared—swallowed up in darkness!

Abby gripped the window frame. *Oh, what am I supposed to do?*

Suddenly a scary voice came out of the night. "Jump, Abby! Jump!" It was Luke trying to holler in a whisper. Just then, the rope that tied the skiff to the ship went slack. Captain Chandler had cut the boat's tow line free of the mutineers, leaving Abby at their mercy.

Swallowing hard, Abby climbed up on the window seat and put one leg through the opened window. She realized that the captain and Luke could see her because of the backlight of the cabin's lantern. If she wanted off the ship, she would have to jump into the unknown—into black water as scary as her nightmares, where unseen things waited to rise from the deep and grab her.

Abby held the window frame and pulled her other leg through. Her weight now rested on the frame. All she had to do was push off, and she would be free of the ship and free of Jackal.

Oh, God, I'm so scared. Help me. She could barely make out the water twenty feet below.

A pounding on the cabin door jerked Abby from her misery. "Open the door!" Mr. Job cried. She could hear other men with him. Then the most frightening sound of all: a key in the lock.

Abby's heart beat so fast she thought it might explode. The door flew open, and Mr. Job with two others burst into the room.

Abby pushed off and flew through space. When she hit the sea, she went down briefly in the cold water. Then she rose to the surface, sputtering. Her clothes weighed her down.

"Luke!" she screamed. *Where is the skiff?*

The waves sloshed over her head, but she struck out swimming in the direction she'd last seen the skiff.

"Abby, over here!" Luke's voice sounded panicked. Behind her, Abby could tell a lantern was spilling golden light on the waves. Water smacked her in the face. *Someone must be hanging a lantern out of the window. They're searching for me!*

In the glow of the lantern, the waves lightened to

green. And out of the watery deep came a powerful form that shot past her like lightning.

Abby's heart almost stopped. *Shark! A giant, fast shark!* It was so close, she'd felt the water turbulence as it passed.

Panic swamped Abby's mind. She flailed and fought against the sea, trying to catch her breath. Waves seemed intent on dunking her, but she could hear Luke screaming her name. Men from the ship were yelling, too. Then she heard a splash, and a moment later, a gunshot.

They were shooting at her!

A sudden splashing in front of her made her stop swimming. She screamed. Then Luke's hand reached out and grabbed her wrist. There was no time for words. He pulled her toward the skiff— now only yards away.

Captain Chandler's strong arms gripped Abby and lifted her in. Luke threw one leg over the gunwale, glancing back over his shoulder. Then he, too, fell safely in the skiff, sending it dipping in the swells. "Captain, they shot at us!"

Captain Chandler shook his head. "No, boy. Mr. Job took aim at the shark. I believe he hit it, too. Otherwise, one of you might not be here."

Abby shivered on the wooden bench. The skiff rocked in the waves as Captain Chandler removed his blue wool coat and draped it around her. She drew the coat close. "Thank you, Captain, but they know we're here. They'll be after us soon."

"We'll know in a few minutes if they're coming," the captain said. "But let's take a moment to thank God for your safe escape from the ship."

Luke sat next to Abby. "And the shark," he said quietly.

The captain bowed his head, speaking softly to God. Abby closed her eyes, tears squeezing out. She wanted to lie down and sleep and forget about all of her problems and fears. Wearily, she leaned against Luke's shoulder and sighed. His arm found its way around her back. When the captain stopped praying, Abby thought she would just keep her eyes closed and rest awhile. Then Luke spoke up, hesitantly at first. "I haven't talked to You, God, since Ma died. And I feel bad about that. I'm . . . real sorry. I just want to thank You for . . . keeping Abby safe from that shark. I was sure it was gonna get her. . . ."

The waves rhythmically hit the gunwales of the skiff, but all Abby could hear was Luke's voice cracking with emotion. She opened her eyes and saw Luke's face covered by his one free hand. She let go of the captain's coat and tenderly placed her palm against Luke's cheek.

Captain Chandler cleared his throat. "In the meantime, I don't intend to make it easy for those mutineers to get us. Let's hoist our own sail, Luke, and set our course for Oahu." He rose to retrieve the short mast and sail tucked under the benches. "With a little nudge from God, we just might get her pointed in the right direction and make landfall by morning. Right, son?"

Luke rose to help. "Aye, sir."

Abby gathered the coat tighter about her and closed her eyes. Gratitude swept over her. They were lost at sea again, but this time with an ocean-going captain who knew currents and sailing. As she took a deep breath and opened her eyes, she was struck by the beauty of the night. The stars shone brightly from the rich black canopy—like diamonds in a velvet-lined jewelry case. She remembered how God had told her, *I WILL WATCH OVER YOU LIKE THE ANCIENT STARS*. The memory of His words soothed her.

Luke and Captain Chandler spoke together as they raised the mast and hoisted the sail. She heard Luke point out the ship's lanterns, far in the distance, as he said, "We're not worth the bother of them turning around."

Abby smiled. No doubt Jackal considered himself well rid of the bad-luck girl. He didn't want any reminders of God onboard. Or perhaps he hadn't awakened yet, and the crew didn't care about them.

Abby soon quit listening to Captain Chandler and Luke. Her heart was too full to listen to human words. For the first time in her life, she had heard Luke talk to God, the One in whom she now had a greater trust.

The chambers of her heart were ringing like a bell

tower, chiming with joy even in the midst of being lost on the wide sea.

Wrapped in the captain's coat, Abby slept off her exhaustion on the wooden bench. When dawn broke, she sat up in the light pouring over a distant mountain.

"Land!" she shouted, as if she had just discovered it.

Captain Chandler grinned at Luke. "Good thing she's onboard, or we might have missed it." He winked, and Luke grinned back at him from his place at the tiller.

"Crinoline corsets! I just thought you'd like to know," she said with a harrumph.

"Don't get a bee in your bonnet, Abby," Luke said. "We're glad you got your beauty sleep. Captain figures we'll be ashore in the next half hour or so."

"We're on the windward side of the island, so we've had full sails all morning. Hold her steady, Luke," the captain said, "and we'll beach at that distant stretch of sand. If I recollect things correctly, that might be Kailua up ahead."

"Why, Kailua is where my uncle's ranch is," Abby said happily. "We could see Ma and Pa today!"

"Could happen," the captain agreed. "But the

whole area is called Kailua, if I'm not mistaken. You say he owns some land around there?"

Abby rubbed the sleepy seeds from her eyes and spoke enthusiastically. "Yes, a whole ranch! I believe he's rich, at least in land."

Luke spoke up. "Ab, you thirsty?"

"Powerfully thirsty, and a little hungry, too."

The captain reached over to a wooden box near Luke and lifted the lid. He took out a tin box and a glass jar full of water. "It's not much, but soda crackers and water are better than hunger and thirst."

Abby ate gratefully.

As the minutes sped by, they sailed over the sea swells. A half mile from shore, a frolicking school of dolphins greeted them. The joyful animals leapt and twirled from the sea, enjoying themselves as they splashed backward into the water. Small geysers of spray shot up where they reentered the water.

"Oh, Luke! Aren't they beautiful?" Abby cooed. "I'd never be afraid to swim in the ocean if I had dolphins with me."

The captain replied, "They are wondrous creatures—and always a good omen to sailors and Hawaiians."

Escorting them toward the beach, the dolphins took turns swimming at the bow of the skiff, diving just ahead of it. When the little boat finally was within thirty yards of the white shore, the dolphins veered off and headed back out to sea.

"Farewell!" Abby called.

"At least there's no coral reef here!" Luke shouted over the sound of crashing waves.

Abby remembered their first landing, but this time the boat was tossed onto the gently sloping beach. It ran smoothly with the breaking wave before coming to a halt. Luke and Abby leapt out ahead of the captain and helped push the boat onto dry sand.

In the early morning light, Abby spied a group of women and a cluster of grass huts in the distance. "Shall we go ask for directions?" she asked.

"Lead on," Captain Chandler said.

As they drew near, they were greeted by a large Hawaiian woman with long white hair and a beautiful round face. "*Aloha, haoles!* Welcome to Kailua." The islander sat on a grass mat, mending a huge fishing net spread out before her. Three other large women, working on the same net, raised friendly faces to them.

Delighted, Abby spoke. "*Aloha.* I am Abby, and this is Luke and Captain Chandler. His crew mutinied, we escaped, and now we're looking for my parents. They should be at my uncle's ranch here in Kailua."

The woman who had greeted them rose, her hair swinging below her waist. She stood tall, regal, and proud. "I am Olani, a chieftess of Kailua." She spoke in a singsong voice, her face gracious and kind. "Little *wahine* has much story to say. Come.

You refresh to my home; eat *pu-pus*—some papaya and fish. Then my son take you for uncle's home." She motioned for the other women to come with them.

Abby's mouth dropped open. "You're Olani?"

When Olani smiled, the corners of her eyes crinkled. "Yes. You hear of me?"

"Your son, Kimo, told me about you. He said you have hair like the mountain mists." Abby grew more excited by the minute. "Is Kimo here?"

"He up-country for his father, hunting. They be back today. You will see him, I think."

"I'd love to wait for him," Abby said anxiously, "but my parents . . . think I'm dead—lost at sea—and we have to leave right away for my uncle's ranch. Do you know where Samuel Kendall lives?"

Olani put down her wooden mending needle. "Yes, but miles from here—up *pali, mauka,* toward the mountains." She pointed to the distant mountain southwest of the village. "You leave now. You make before sunset. Pack water and food."

Abby's face showed her disappointment. "Oh. I'd hoped we'd see them soon."

Luke spoke up. "How's the climb, Miss Olani? Is it rough?"

"Miss Olani think you *haole* boy have no problem to climb up. Abby has good strong legs too?"

Abby swallowed. "Well, if I can rest a lot, I can make it." *But I'm already tired.*

Olani looked at her knowingly. "I think you take

my horse, Sugar. She climb mountain good. She carry pack, too. You little bitty thing. She carry Abby, no problem."

Abby brightened. "Oh, Olani, thank you so much." Without thinking, she threw her arms about the large chieftess.

"Come, *haole* girl." With that, Olani and her large friends smiled blissfully. It seemed to Abby they had not a care in the world. And with their help, neither would she.

Two hours later Abby was riding Sugar, while Luke and Captain Chandler walked ahead of her.

Though tired from the long night, the three had eaten a delicious breakfast of papaya and fish, as well as coconut, baked breadfruit, and coconut milk. They had been strengthened for their journey not only by the food but also by Olani's lilting voice of kindness. After Olani had given them expert directions, Abby, Luke, and Captain Chandler had started their trek up the mountain.

"She is truly worthy of her title of chieftess," Captain Chandler said as they marched through a thicket of scrub and kiave. "Such loving-kindness—'*aloha* spirit' they call it." He shook his head in seeming amazement. "You won't find that in many other places around the world."

"Yep," Luke agreed. "If my Aunt Dagmar had even one little fingerful of *aloha,* I could have stayed there four more years."

Abby's mind had moved away from Olani's beach home and the comfort she'd found there. She was looking ahead to her reunion with Ma and Pa, even little Sarah. Tears welled up regularly as she thought about seeing their amazed faces. To them, she'd be back from the grave! *Oh, this will be a happy day!* she thought.

As the flat land began to rise along with the sun, all talking stopped. Occasionally the travelers stopped to drink deeply from the goatskin bag of water.

Abby had long since given back to Captain Chandler his coat, now tied behind Sugar's saddle. No one had noticed the flattened leather scroll inside Abby's dress, but in the heat, it was beginning to itch and scratch. Since Sugar walked behind the two men, Abby took the opportunity to unbutton her top button and remove the map. *But what should I do with it?* Her gaze fell on the captain's coat tied behind Sugar's saddle. She quickly tied the map to the back of Sugar's saddle and covered it with the captain's coat.

As they pressed on, low shrubbery gave way to trees, both light and dark green. Captain Chandler gestured toward a pale-green leafed tree with large brown nuts. "Abby," he said, turning to look at her, "that is a kukui tree, sometimes called a *candlenut*. We are about to enter a kukui forest I think."

Luke inclined his head toward a dark green tree up ahead. "What's that one called, Captain?"

"It's known as a koa tree. The two trees often grow together at this elevation. They make a pretty contrast to each other, don't you think?"

Luke snorted. "I s'pose so. That's Abby's interest—drawing trees and birds and such. Personally, I don't pay it much mind."

Abby smiled. "You never know when it'll come in handy, knowing about local flora and fauna, Luke."

"She's right, boy. A man who knows about his surroundings can master them. For example, the sweet-smelling sandalwood trees that grow on the Hawaiian mountains are worth a fortune right now." The captain paused and shook his head. "And my fortune is on its way to China without me."

"Why don't we stop, Captain," Abby said, in an effort to cheer him, "and fortify ourselves with the lunch Olani prepared for us?"

Luke let out a whoop. "Great idea, Ab!"

The weary travelers stepped off the beaten track into a shaded grove of kukui trees and opened the packed basket. They laid out their lunch of fruit, broiled fish, and chicken. Forty minutes later, after a short nap, they were back on the trail again. The

sun was strong and hot, but they often moved
under clumps of shady forest trees. Not long after
lunch, they came upon an outcropping of rocks and
a cliff overlooking blue-green Kailua Bay below.

Captain Chandler rolled up his white shirtsleeves
and raised his face to the trade winds. "I never tire
of the sea," he said. "Look at the ship yonder under
full sail. She's a beauty. . . ." His voice stopped as his
eyebrows narrowed. He watched the distant ship
intently, then cried, "By the saints! That's *my* ship!
It's the *Flying Lady* returning!"

Luke came alongside him, shielding the sun from
his eyes. "You're right, Captain. But why would
they come back here after sailing on hours ago?"

Abby chewed her lower lip nervously as she
dismounted. In a moment, she joined them. "I . . .
uh . . . think I know why they've returned. . . ."

"You?" sputtered the captain. "Well, for heaven's
sake, girl, spit it out!"

Abby untied the rolled leather map from beneath
the saddle and held it up. "I have Jackal's treasure
map. It's only a little bit damp."

The captain took it from her while Luke
whooped, doing a little jig in the dirt near the cliff.
"Man alive!" he enthused. "You hornswaggled that
varmint! What a great trick, Abby!"

The captain did not look at the map. Instead, he
rolled it and handed it back to her. "I hardly think
having twenty armed men on our tail is 'great.'"

Luke pressed on, oblivious to the captain's thoughts. "How'd you ever do it, Ab?"

Abby blushed, her cheeks looking like two ripe apples. "Well . . . when Jackal told me he was going to send you to the bilge, Captain, and tie me to the galley, I knew we'd never get a chance to escape. So I . . . uh . . . smacked him on the head."

Luke hooted with pleasure. "What'd you use, Ab?"

"I . . . uh . . . used the peppershaker."

For a moment no one spoke. Then Captain Chandler broke into a chuckle that turned into a rumbling laugh. Everyone joined in.

When the merriment died down, the Captain wiped his eyes and said, "Well, I'll be . . . with the peppershaker my lovely Isobel bought me, you say? She knows how I love my seasonings! She will be delighted to hear it, Abby."

"Then what happened, Abby?" Luke asked.

"Well, I took off for the door, but I began to worry that maybe I'd done him in, so I snuck back to see if he was still breathing."

"Abby, that was brave!" Luke gazed at her with pride.

Abby, pleased with the compliment, continued. "That's when I saw the map sticking out of his shirtfront, and for some reason, I just took it! Between the whack on the head and all the rum he'd been drinking, he probably didn't wake up until this morning."

"Bravo, Abby!" The captain's eyes shone. "Thank the Good Lord He got you through it. . . ." He stroked his chin, deep in thought. "When he finally came to, I bet Jackal howled in rage. He's returned for the map. And when he sees the ship's skiff on the beach, he'll know we're here. But we have the element of surprise on our side." He stared at his distant vessel. "Perhaps we can use it to our advantage." He motioned for Abby and Luke to sit on the rocks beside him.

"Let's plan our move. First off, Jackal will come ashore, and he might learn where we're heading. Abby, do you want him to know where your family lives?"

"No, sir," Abby said, her voice concerned.

"Nor do I," said the captain. "Then here is what we must do: We must return to the beach and ask for Olani's help. Perhaps we can secure some local *kanaka*—Hawaiian men—to help us."

Luke's eyebrows raised. "If Jackal and his men come after us, how are they gonna know we went back down the mountain?"

Abby spoke up, full of enthusiasm. "Oh, we must leave clues—through the kukui groves—so they follow them."

"Good thinking, Abby. Yes, we can leave bits of cloth, broken twigs—things like that. By the time they realize we've returned to the beach, we'll be way ahead of them!"

They hurried off the path and cut through the

kukui forest. There they left shreds of cloth hanging from shrubs, plenty of footprints in the dirt, and broken branches to mark their passing. But all the while, Abby had a plan of her own taking shape in her imagination.

Chapter Seventeen

For several hours, Abby, Luke, and Captain Chandler worked their way down the mountain through groves of kukui and koa. By the time they sighted Olani's village, the sun had set, and another full moon was rising.

As they drew near Olani's home, set back from the beach, Sugar neighed loudly. Although torches and a few fires burned in the village, the light of the moon was so bright that Abby could see clearly. There, anchored a hundred feet from shore, was the *Flying Lady*, occupied by the mutineers.

Abby dismounted and led Sugar toward Olani's house. The captain and Luke walked behind. As they approached Olani's open door, Sugar neighed again. Through the doorframe stepped a large Hawaiian man. He almost collided with Abby.

Peering closely at her, his face was transformed by joy. "It is you, little *wahine?*" Kimo beamed at her.

"Kimo! How good it is to see a familiar face! Are my mother and father all right?"

He came up to Abby and bent down, rubbing her nose with his own. Abby knew this was the customary greeting of love between Hawaiians, and she was warmed by the gesture. The large man stepped back. "You return to us from sleep of death. Kimo told you storm coming!"

Abby laughed. "I'll never doubt your nose again, Kimo!"

His handsome features held a look of deep satisfaction. "Your parents, they will know much joy soon," he said.

"Oh, Kimo, it's good to hear of them. Did they go to my uncle's ranch?"

"Yes, *wahine*. They are there with little *wahine*, Sarah. I call her Noe, 'The Mist.' Her white hair like Olani's, my royal mother."

Captain Chandler stepped forward then, and Abby introduced him. "The captain was going to give us a ride here, but his men mutinied, Kimo, all because one man had a treasure map. We barely escaped with our lives. Jackal wanted to kill us all— or sell us into slavery!"

Kimo scowled. "I think we teach lesson for this Jackal. Olani met him today when the ship dropped anchor here. He is much rude. We worried when he followed your trail. But now, I think we plan a *nui*—big welcome for him."

"That's just what I had in mind," Captain Chandler said.

"Kimo," Abby added, "this is Luke, my friend from California. He was a stowaway on your ship."

Kimo's eyes widened. "You tricked us?" he said to Luke.

"Yes, sir. I'm sorry," Luke said, scuffing his shoe in the dirt.

Kimo's smile evaporated. "Abby, you join Olani. I want to take Captain to meet my friends. Together we fix things quick like. You, Luke, come with us. We soon see if you are as good a fighter as you are a 'hider.'"

Poor Luke! Abby thought, but she was still glad to have Kimo on their side.

Olani welcomed Abby into her home. Although it was a large grass house on the outside, inside it was beautifully decorated with hand-carved furniture from Boston. There was a dining table, graced with a white-and-gold tea set. In a nearby corner stood a china hutch. In the opposite corner a mahogany rolltop desk with a quill and inkwell stood near a lovely four-poster bed with a red silk coverlet.

"Abby rest here," Olani said, pointing to the luxurious bed.

"Oh, no, Olani, I couldn't. That's your bed."

Olani only laughed. "No, this be guest bed. I use sleeping mat like always. Old way die hard."

"I'm too excited to sleep right now, Olani, but could I sit at your desk for a bit?"

"Ah, you know to read and write?"

"Yes." An idea had formed in Abby's mind. She smiled as she thought about how to get it on paper.

"Good, I get you *tapa* for work on. It like paper. Use ink on desk. Olani be back soon."

After Olani returned with the brown *tapa*, she left Abby alone. Abby rubbed the *tapa* between her fingers. It was almost as soft as silk, but it rustled like paper. She dipped the quill in the ink and bent over the *tapa*. While she worked, she heard Olani return with her friends. They rolled out their sleeping mats under the stars at the hut's entrance.

When Abby's eyes grew heavy from her task, she rose and made her way to the bed. She sighed as she sank onto the red silk coverlet, which was more beautiful than any she had ever had at home. Then she trimmed the oil lamp on the bedstand and the hut was thrown into darkness. Abby sank into the plush pillows and was soon lulled to sleep.

Three hours passed as Captain Chandler, Kimo, and Luke prepared their surprise. They moved through the sleeping village, waking the strongest and bravest men Kimo knew. He had told the captain that

Jackal had left the ship with five crewmen. That meant fourteen men were left onboard. They decided to hike a mile to another village to raise up an army of twenty strong warriors.

Gathering silently on Kailua Beach, the brave *kanaka* tied their loincloths tightly about them. Captain Chandler and Luke removed their shirts and shoes. Each man unsheathed his knife and clenched it between his teeth as he slipped into the moon-frosted sea and swam toward the anchored ship.

The water felt cool to Luke initially, but it soon became refreshing. It would have been an enjoyable swim, he thought, but for the fact that blood might soon be shed. He hoped it wouldn't be his! Kimo had given him a dagger, but he'd never fought a man before.

When the twenty *kanaka*, who were used to swimming these waters, reached the ship a bit ahead of Luke and Captain Chandler, they gathered around the anchor chain at the bow of the ship. The anchor line stayed taut, but the ship bobbed up and down.

The captain removed the knife from his mouth and whispered, "I'll go up the chain first, so if there's trouble, it will fall on me." He gripped the blade between his teeth again and began to pull himself up the cable.

Water splashed off the captain as he climbed up, and Luke cringed. He hoped no one had heard as he followed the captain, clinging to the slippery chain with both his fingers and toes.

Suddenly he saw a glow of light moving toward the bow of the ship. Luke could see Captain Chandler hadn't yet noticed. Had someone heard them?

Just then, a lantern shone off the bow, revealing the captain and Luke in a dripping, awkward pose.

"Cap'n, is that ye?" questioned Mr. Job. The light reflecting on his face showed raised white eyebrows.

The captain, unable to do more than grunt, pierced his first mate with eagle eyes.

Mr. Job's white eyebrows drew together in astonishment as he glanced over the captain and saw the many *kanaka* treading water below. "Why, by the grace of the Almighty, ye've come to reclaim yer ship, sir!" Mr. Job doused the light. "Come 'round to the gangway, Cap'n, and I'll be lettin' down the rope ladder." He hurried away.

Most of the men swam around to midship, but Captain Chandler kept climbing. Luke followed him. When their feet touched the deck, the captain took the blade from his mouth and motioned Luke to crouch down.

The deck was empty. Mr. Job had not given them away. A moment later, the Hawaiians climbed onto the deck, dripping but silent. The captain and Luke joined them, and they spoke in whispers.

"Mr. Job, where are the men?" Captain Chandler asked.

"Sleeping off another binge, sir. And never have I been so glad to have a crew drunk!"

The captain placed a hand on Mr. Job's shoulder. "Well done, Job," he said quietly.

"Sir, two of the men—Smithers and Woodruff—have come to me complainin' about Jackal. They said they wished there'd been a way to give ye back yer ship. I think we can count on them, sir."

Captain Chandler paused. "When we come upon them, we'll see their reaction. If they fight us, it's to the brig with them, but if they support us, I'll reinstate them."

Just as Luke came up behind the captain and Mr. Job, a head peered out of the forward hatch.

Instinctively, Luke grabbed the wooden bucket nearby and jammed it over the sailor's head. A muffled scream erupted from under the bucket, but Luke grabbed the drunken sailor by the shirt and dragged him up through the hatch.

The captain and the Hawaiians rushed over. Within seconds, the salty dog hit the deck with a thud and was immediately bound with ropes and gagged.

The captain clapped Luke on the back. "Good job, Luke!"

Kimo looked on appreciatively. "Not bad for a *haole* boy who stows away!"

Luke warmed to the praise and adventure. "Let's go get the rest of the sea dogs!" he said enthusiastically.

Twenty-three grins shone in the moonlight as the captain led the way down the hatch.

Chapter Eighteen

Abby came out of her sleep feeling troubled. For a moment she could not remember where she was. Then she remembered: She was in Olani's home. Luke and Captain Chandler were on their way to take back the ship.

Suddenly she heard Olani's voice outside the hut, speaking with authority. "You go. Be gone!"

"By thunder, ye'll learn respect!" An angry voice boomed beyond the open door of the hut.

It's Jackal!

When his ornery voice receded as he stormed off with his men, Abby moved slowly through the dark grass hut. She tried desperately to remember where the table and chairs were.

Reaching the doorway, she peeked out and saw six men marching away. They were heading toward the beach. One of them carried a torch. When they disappeared behind a small sand dune, Abby hurried out to Olani, who stood watching them, her arms folded across her massive chest.

"Olani, that was Jackal!" Abby's braid had come loose hours before. Her thick curly hair stuck out in all directions.

Olani turned to her, and the scowl on her face was transformed to gentleness. "Our little *wahine* has Hawaiian hair," she said, tenderly laying a hand on Abby's curls. Abby smiled at Olani and her friends.

"I know he is the Jackal that take ship and treat you bad," Olani said. "But the men go for meet him with *nui*—big surprise. His time is near."

Abby swallowed hard. "But how do we know the captain's surprise is ready for him? Shouldn't we slow him down?"

Olani looked thoughtful, as one of her dark-haired friends, Kaalani, reached out and touched Abby's curls. "'*Nani*-hair.' That mean pretty hair," she explained to Abby. Then Kaalani turned to the rest of her friends. "Abby be right. We can slow those bad men down."

"We go," Olani commanded.

Abby and the four women hurried through the village and onto the sand dune, following Jackal and his men. Abby's stomach churned with dread. She didn't want to face that devil again.

As they reached the top of the rise, Olani broke into a run. Abby's mouth dropped open at the speed with which the large woman moved. Her companions followed suit, and Abby tried to keep up.

The men were heading to a skiff, which had been beached near Olani's fishing nets.

"Jaaa-ckal!" Olani's voice carried over the sand, stopping the men in their tracks.

Abby and the women were only fifteen feet from the men. The man holding the torch was Spandler, Jackal's right-hand man. "Ignore 'em!" she heard him mutter. "I want me rum and a good sleep. I'm sick of Hawaiians."

But Jackal turned toward Olani, his shirtsleeves tight where the muscles of his arms bulged. He grinned wickedly as he waited for her to catch up. "No, it's been awhile since I taught such a sassy woman a lesson."

Olani stood tall in her muumuu, her long white hair trailing off her shoulders. She strode toward him. "Me think you mo' better stay here. That itty-bitty boat not yours for use."

Jackal only sneered, his black eyes glittering with eagerness. "Try to stop me, big *wahine*."

For a moment, the only noise besides the crashing waves was the in-drawn breath of Olani's friends, who were shocked by the disrespect shown to their royal chieftess. Abby came running up in time to see Olani catch Jackal off guard as she backhanded him. His head flew back at the impact, almost knocking him down. Abby could see by the light of Spandler's torch a look of amazed anger spreading across Jackal's contorted features. "Uh-oh," she whispered.

Jackal came up swinging, but Olani ducked. With her head lowered, she rammed Jackal in the stomach. Her momentum and weight shot him backward onto the sand.

Abby's eyes went wide as she watched Olani get the best of Jackal. Suddenly Abby gave a terrified yelp as someone latched onto her hair from behind.

"Gotcha, ye little cur," Spandler said as he dropped the torch and grabbed her. He began dragging her off toward the skiff.

Abby tried to put up a fight, but she was no match. "Olani!" she wailed.

The chieftess left the fallen Jackal as she rushed to Abby's aid, tackling Spandler from behind. His knees buckled and he fell hard, letting go of Abby's hair.

One of Olani's friends had seated herself on top of Jackal, who was cussing up a storm. But it was no use; he couldn't budge the three-hundred-pound woman off his back. Abby grinned as she watched Olani's friend wave his pistol at him.

The other four sailors looked on in distress. None of them had ever considered mutiny before Jackal had shown up, and none of them had ever struck a woman before. They were unwilling to start now. But two of them approached the woman seated on Jackal and tried to lift her off. They weren't getting very far. And neither were the two men who tried to pry Olani and another woman off Spandler.

Abby rubbed her sore head where Spandler had yanked her hair. She frantically thought of what to do next. Spying the fishing net just twenty feet away, she ran over and picked up yards of it in her thin arms. With all her strength, she began dragging it toward Spandler.

Kaalani darted toward the fishing hut and picked up a long object that shone white in the moonlight. Abby watched her sneak up behind the two men bothering her friends who sat on top of Spandler. *Whack! Crack!* She struck each man on the back of the head. They toppled over.

When she noticed Abby struggling with her load, she hurried over and helped her drag the heavy net to Spandler. The two women rose from his back, and he flipped over, ready to rise. "Me no think you should," said the woman brandishing her club. Spandler sank back down on the sand in dismay. And the three *wahine* threw the net over him and his two fallen friends.

Then Kaalani went over to help her friend who sat on Jackal. The *wahine* needed little help, for she had a firm grip on Jackal's pistol and was brandishing it at the two sailors who were trying to come to his aid.

"Hey, bring de big mouth here!" shouted Olani. Kaalani went over with her club and helped herd Jackal and his two men to the net. "Get!" she ordered, raising the net on one end. When Jackal's expression showed he wasn't going to obey, the other *wahine* raised the pistol and took aim on him.

With open mouth and utter disbelief on his face,

Jackal obeyed. The net was tossed over him and his friends, and then Olani and the three other Hawaiian women sat down on each corner. "They think two times before they insult Olani again!" crowed Kaalani.

Abby's mouth tugged at the corners. She had never seen such a funny sight in her life. She began to giggle, and the Hawaiian women joined in.

Ah, such a wonderful feeling of friendship! Abby thought. *I love these Hawaiian people. They are the best I've ever met.*

"Kaalani, what is that club thing you were using?" Abby asked.

Kaalani held up her long object in the moonlight. "This be the jawbone of a big dolphin. He used it to ram his enemy the shark—and so do we!" The women chuckled again, while Jackal and his men squirmed under their net enclosure.

"Go to sleep, little men," Olani crooned. "You will need it, I think. Soon Kimo will come for you."

"I wonder how Luke is doing," Abby said to no one in particular.

Olani glanced at her and smiled. "If he be half as brave as you, Nani-hair, he make fine warrior."

As Abby sat on the net in the moonlight and soft Kailua sand, she thought Olani might just be right. At any rate, it wasn't polite to disagree with a royal chieftess. That was a mistake Jackal would probably not make again!

When Kaalani began to hum softly, Olani said,

"Nani-hair, go get for us the drum gourd by the hut." Abby rose to retrieve the large gourd she remembered seeing earlier.

Now while the women waited for sunrise, Kaalani began to beat the drum, and Olani joined in with a chant. Abby listened to the beautiful Hawaiian words that floated from the women's lips. The drumbeat pulsed like a heartbeat—the heartbeat of Hawaii, Abby realized.

And when they began to teach her an ancient chant of victory, Abby's own heart swelled with joy. *These people are easy to love,* she mused. *Their aloha spirit makes Hawaii feel like home.*

Chapter Nineteen

When morning dawned, Hawaiians from the village joined them on the beach and enjoyed a good laugh at the sight of six big men trapped under a net by their chieftess and her friends.

Kimo and two of his friends had swum in and were ready to row the mutineers back to the ship so they could be jailed in the brig.

"*Wahine* warrior," he said to Abby as he sat down in the sand next to her. "Your stowaway boy, he be a warrior, too."

Abby was thrilled to hear about Luke's part in the retaking of the ship. He had fought with his fists and subdued the drunken sailors with the others. But Kimo didn't spend long on it. "Let's get the men to the ship. They deserve a nice visit to Honolulu fort," he said with a mischievous grin.

Surrounded by natives, Jackal and the sailors obeyed the command to get in the skiff being held steady in the surf by three *kanaka*. Abby climbed in the back next to Kimo, who kept the pistol trained on Jackal. "So," he teased, "you met *wahine* warriors—and lost!"

Jackal, Abby thought, looked as mad as a wild dog.

Two of Jackal's sailors were ordered to row the skiff toward the *Flying Lady* as a dozen Hawaiians swam out with them. Captain Chandler came to the railing and hailed the approaching skiff. "Abby, well done!" he shouted.

The rope ladder was lowered, and the Hawaiian swimmers joined their friends on deck. As the skiff neared the ship, the sailors drew in the oars. One by one, the mutineers rose and clambered aboard. Jackal was the last to go.

Just before he left the rowboat, he gave Abby a look that chilled her to the bone. "I'll remember ye for this!" Then he swore and clambered up the ladder.

As Kimo tossed a line to Mr. Job to secure the skiff, Abby began the climb up the ladder. Her legs were shaking from exhaustion. The lack of sleep, the lack of food, and the excitement were all catching up with her.

One by one, Spandler and the other sailors were being carted off, bound in ropes, belowdecks to the brig, which was really the wet, smelly hold of the ship. But Jackal was still being tied with his hands behind his back, so he watched as Abby struggled up the ladder on shaking legs.

Captain Chandler reached out a hand to help

Abby up, but she didn't take it. Instead, she reached in her dress front and began to pull out the leather map that she'd recently hidden there.

She almost laughed when she saw Jackal's eyes widen with recognition.

"Captain," Abby said, as she hung by one hand on the ladder, "I want you to take this map, which started the bad luck for you." She lifted it toward the captain's outstretched hand but let go a moment too soon. The captain lunged for the map, but it dropped quickly into the water below and sank into the deep harbor.

"Ye stupid, worthless girl!" Jackal roared. His face contorted in rage, and he lunged toward Abby, though his hands were bound behind him. "I'll git ye!" Spittle flew out of his mouth, landing in his unkempt black beard. Abby shrank back, but the captain turned and said with blazing eyes, "You'll hold your tongue on my ship or pay the price with twenty lashes. You've made enough trouble for one journey, Jackal. Mr. Job, see that he gets chained below, like the animal he is."

Soon, Jackal was safely escorted to the hold by Mr. Job and two *kanaka*.

The captain turned back to Abby. "Come aboard, dear girl. Don't worry about the map. We are, I think, well rid of it."

Abby climbed aboard and together with Luke and the *kanaka* who'd helped the captain, enjoyed a breakfast provided by Olani. She and her friends brought out a canoe loaded with steaming baked breadfruit and Abby's favorite fruits—bananas, papayas, guavas, and star fruit from the lush regions surrounding the sea.

The trade winds cooled off the heat of the rising sun. Flying fish jetted occasionally from the sea, and one of the *kanaka* struck up a ukulele and began entertaining everyone.

Like her stomach, Abby's heart was full. The captain had his ship back, and the twenty *kanaka* had volunteered to sail it to Honolulu for him, along with his loyal crewmates—Mr. Job, Woodruff, and Smithers. Once they got to Honolulu, Jackal and the mutineers would have a home at the stockade. Jackal would never be a threat to her again.

But now Abby couldn't stop thinking of her family. She leaned over and whispered to Luke, "I'll even be happy to sleep with Sarah tonight!" She remembered how often she had complained about Sarah taking all the covers and throwing her leg over Abby in the middle of the night. If God helped her get back to her family, she'd *never* complain about that again.

Olani, who had been moving through the crowd onboard, bent down and put an arm around Abby. "Nani-hair, you ready now for home?"

The love in the regal lady's eyes was more than Abby could bear. It was the kind of unconditional love her mother had, and Abby's eyes flooded with tears. She nodded mutely, and Olani gathered her close.

"I think Sugar take you home, now, little *wahine* warrior. But I think you come back soon."

Abby smiled. "Thank you, Olani. I will, I promise. I'll bring Sugar home in two or three days. Maybe my ma and pa will come with me. I'd love for them to meet you."

Olani hugged her again and then called Kimo over. "Abby and Luke can go on Sugar back up mountain. You take her now to shore."

Kimo bent down and rubbed noses with his royal mother. Olani pressed her palm against his brown cheek fondly.

And then Abby saw Captain Chandler striding toward her.

"Abby, I see you're getting ready to leave."

Until that moment, Abby hadn't realized how much she cared for Captain Chandler. He had been their friend. And he had been so good and kind, so trusting of God in spite of the tragedies he'd experienced. She didn't want their friendship to end.

"I hate to go, Captain, but I need to let my parents know we're alive." She swallowed hard.

"Of course you must leave. I only wish I could accompany you to see your happy reunion. They have much to be proud of in you and Luke."

Captain Chandler called Luke over and pumped

his hand. "I've been proud to serve with you, young man. If you ever need work, I'd be happy to have you onboard anytime."

Luke looked up at him with a genuine smile. "Thank you, sir—for everything."

The captain gave Abby a hug. "Take good care of Luke, Abby. He needs a young woman of character on his side."

Then they were hugging their many new Hawaiian friends, heading down the ladder, and canoeing toward shore. With a basket of food prepared by Kaalani, Abby and Luke mounted Sugar around noon and began to retrace their steps *mauka,* toward the mountain.

Abby fell asleep as soon as they rode past the scrub and headed into the cooler regions of the kukui forests. Honeycreepers sang their distinctive songs, and the trees swayed in the gentle trade winds. Luke held on to Abby as she slept, propped against his chest.

Imagine, he thought. *Abby and those women outwitting Jackal and his rotten gang!* Luke imagined it for a couple of miles as Sugar plodded steadily along the path.

When they got to the overlook where they'd

sighted the *Flying Lady*, Luke woke Abby and the two dismounted.

Walking to the outcropping at the cliff, he pointed. "Look, the ship is leaving. Captain Chandler is finally on his way to Honolulu—and Jackal to prison."

They decided to eat again since it had been four hours since their last meal. Abby watched Luke pick at the food. "What's wrong? Aren't you hungry?"

"Not much. Guess I had my fill."

Abby was growing too excited to eat, as well. "Let's press on. I want to see Ma before tomorrow!"

Once back on the track, however, the steady rhythm of Sugar's gait lulled Abby back to sleep. She had been awake most of the night. Luke had to keep a tight grip on her, as she almost toppled over twice. Worse yet, she snored!

"Gracious, Abby, you sound like a bullfrog." But she didn't hear his complaint.

She only slept through it, leaving Luke to worry alone about their reception. *No doubt they'll be throwing hats in the air when they see Abby, but will they throw me right off the ranch? After all, if Abby hadn't come to the jollyboat the night of the storm, she would never have been lost at sea.* Not only that, Luke knew her parents would want to respect his aunt's wishes. Even if they weren't directly mad at him, would they send him back to Aunt Dagmar?

I won't go, Luke said to himself. *I'd rather find Captain Chandler and work for him!*

As the afternoon crept toward early evening, Abby woke and stretched. "Luke, we're almost there. I can feel it in my bones!" she cried.

Sure enough, within a half hour as the sun set behind the mountain, casting the trail in shadows, Abby and Luke heard the distant sound of someone chopping wood.

Abby sat up straight and clucked to Sugar. "Geddyup, girl," she ordered, and Sugar picked up her tired pace by falling into a bumpy trot.

As they rounded a bend, a fenced-in corral with one horse appeared up ahead. To the left, nestled in a kukui grove, sat a small ranch house with a surrounding porch and smoke rising from the chimney. In the yard, a man stood with his back to them, wiping sweat off his forehead. He held an ax in both hands, which he raised over his head to chop another piece of wood on the chopping block. But before he could bring it crashing down, Abby's voice rang out, "Paaaa!"

Thomas Kendall stopped his swing midair, turned to look over his shoulder, and dropped the ax. His mouth fell open, but no words came forth.

Abby had already leapt from Sugar's back and was running into his open arms.

"Pa!" she choked out. Tears tracked down her dusty cheeks, turning them muddy.

"Abby, oh, Princess," her pa said, lifting her in his arms and burying his head in her shoulder. "Thank God!"

Then he put her down but kept her drawn close to his side with one arm. He tried to shout. "Ma!" he croaked, his throat so choked with emotions he couldn't yell.

Charlotte had already come out on the porch. She stood clinging to the porch post, unable to move, one hand clasped over her mouth. Abby thought she was about to keel over, but Luke jumped from the horse and ran to catch her.

In the nick of time Luke gripped and supported her. Ma clung to him as Abby raced toward her. Then the three held on to each other as if for dear life.

"Oh, Ma!" Abby gasped through her tears, "Ma, I've missed you! I've even missed Sarah."

Her mother's face crumpled as she gave way to happy sobs. "We thought you were dead, but I couldn't quit hoping. Oh, thank the Almighty!" She pushed Abby back to get a good look at her, as if to make sure she was real. Then Ma grasped Abby tightly to her again.

Sarah opened the door of the cabin and stood

stock-still. "Abby," she demanded, "what took you so long to get here?"

Everyone burst into laughter.

"Come on in, kids," said Pa. "We've got a lot of catching up to do." He put his arm around Luke as they walked into the house. Supper smelled inviting.

Chapter Twenty

Long into the night, stories and tales of adventure were shared. Lanterns were lit, the door was left open for a breeze, and Ma kept plying her two lost chicks with food and drink. When she wasn't doing that, she sat next to Abby and held her hand, as if to reassure herself that Abby was really and truly there.

Introductions had been made between Luke and Uncle Samuel, whom Abby had met so long ago that she scarcely remembered him. He looked a lot like Pa but was grayer and thinner. His illness had taken a toll, and when Abby and Luke had gone on a tour of things before darkness settled, they could see the ranch needed many repairs.

Sarah had long since fallen asleep in Pa's lap and been carried to her straw-tick mattress. Around midnight, when Ma went in to check on Sarah, she came back carrying the old cookie tin.

"Captain MacDonald found this on deck the night of the storm." She handed it to Luke. "What's inside is yours, Luke. It's what kept us hoping against hope," she said. "When we saw it, we realized you must have been onboard, hiding in the skiff that broke off in the storm. Every day since, I've prayed the two of you made it safely to land and were on your way back to us." Her eyes were shining with love.

Abby looked at her mother and thought, *The aloha spirit lives in all mothers who love their children.*

Luke opened the tin cover and withdrew the ten-inch carving and his pocketknife. He smiled. "Someday I'll finish this for you, Abby."

Abby inspected the carving. "Why, Luke, it's Sparks, your dog!"

Pa sat up. "Speaking of creatures, there are some that need my attention in the morning. I think it's time we all sacked out, don't you, Ma?"

Ma nodded and gripped Abby's hand firmly. "I'm awfully happy to have you under our roof again, Love."

"Speaking of roofs," Pa said, grinning, "there's work to be done on ours tomorrow. Luke, I'd be grateful for your help, son."

Abby saw Luke take a deep, contented breath. *He knows we need him!*

But Pa continued. "In the next few days, Luke, we'll write Dagmar and let her know you're here. I don't want anyone to ever go through what Abby's ma and I have been through."

Luke bowed his head. "Yes, sir."

"Don't despair, son. It'll take two or three months for letters to go back and forth—maybe longer if the Lord wills it."

Everyone laughed then, and each headed to bed: Abby and Sarah in a tiny room off the kitchen, and Luke to a straw-tick mattress in the front room.

Later that night Sarah, still sound asleep, snuggled up to Abby and tossed one leg over her sister's, as if to keep her close. Satisfaction poured through Abby. "Thank You, God," she murmured before she fell asleep.

Abby woke to the smell of coffee brewing and the sound of her mother humming in the kitchen. The sun had been up a couple of hours already. Then she heard hammering. *Pa must be up on the roof working,* she thought to herself.

As she entered the kitchen, she saw Ma was heating water for her and had put the old copper washtub out. "You said you'd love a bath, so I got it started for you."

Abby had her first bath in over a month with hot water and some of Ma's special lilac soap. She dressed in clean clothes from her trunk and felt like a princess. While she pampered herself, Uncle Samuel fed Sugar for Abby and watered all the horses. Then, racked with weakness, he retired to his room for a long nap.

"He was even worse when we got here," Ma said over an afternoon break as they sat alone at the kitchen table. "Things are in a sad state of disrepair." She shook her head as she glanced at all the clutter Abby's biologist uncle had collected over the years.

"What is it, Ma? Pa can fix all these things with Luke's help."

Ma stirred sugar into her cold coffee. "It's not that, Abby. It's the Great Mahele."

"What's that?"

"The king has finally agreed to let the common people here buy their own land. For the first time in the history of the islands, some of the land won't belong to the king. Until now, most of the islanders were like servants to him, and he owned everything."

"Just like in ancient Europe under the feudal system?" Abby asked, amazed. "The common people were like serfs?"

"That's right. Well, now they can purchase the land they've lived on, which is very kind of the king. But there's one problem. They have to pay the king a quarter of its value."

"Why is that so bad? It sounds like a good deal."

"A lot of the chiefs and royalty are well-off, and they can easily purchase large tracts of land. But most of the common people can't. And I'm afraid your uncle's illness has taken all his money. He can't afford to buy back the land he was given by the king years ago."

"Oh, no!" Abby sighed heavily. *Are we going to have to move again?* "What if we sell some of his cattle?" she asked.

"He's already sold most of his herd just to survive this last year. There's nothing left."

She didn't have to tell Abby they were broke, too. They couldn't help poor Uncle Samuel, for they had come here not only to help him physically but also to share in his land wealth. Now that land was slipping away from them.

Abby didn't know what to say to cheer her mother, so she picked up the broom and started sweeping the whole house. *At least I can help in small ways.* It was the first time in her life she didn't complain about sweeping. In fact, she was glad for the chance to do something for the mother who loved her so much.

Later she helped Ma prepare a simple supper of beans, baked potatoes, and salt pork. Luke and Sarah didn't know the seriousness of the family's financial situation, so dinner was another happy time of tale swapping and joke telling. Uncle Samuel got out his banged-up guitar and strummed a few tunes, which everyone sang.

But that night Abby couldn't sleep well.

Chapter Twenty-One

Abby rose early, when the first hint of dawn appeared. She dressed in her blue cotton button-down and woke Luke, who lay snoring in the front room.

"Come on, you old bullfrog," Abby whispered.

He sat up and rubbed his eyes. "Me? You should've heard yourself when we rode up here on Sugar. I'm surprised your parents didn't hear you coming. Guess they figured it was an approaching thunderstorm."

Abby slugged him playfully on the shoulder. "Come on. We can argue outdoors."

He jumped up, already clothed since he'd slept in his pants and shirt, and followed her out the door. She went on by the corral and headed into the woods, passing fragrant plumeria trees, red hibiscus, and yellow ginger that were just beginning to gain their color in the dawning light.

When she found the cliff overlooking a sleeping

valley, Abby stopped and sat down, dangling her legs over the edge.

"Well, here's the news. There's this new law called the Great Mahele. I guess it's a good thing in the long run because the islanders will get to buy their land from the king. But the bad thing is, my uncle has to purchase his land now, too, even though it was given to him by the king a few years ago. In the past, a new king could take away his land, but once it's bought and registered, it will be his for life."

Luke glanced at her in the honey light of the sunrise. "What's so bad about that?"

She turned to him. "He doesn't have any money, and neither do my parents. That means he'll lose his land if someone else comes in to buy it."

"Oh, no."

"Exactly! We just got here, and I don't want to go back to California—not now. I love Hawaii!" She spoke with so much enthusiasm that Luke chuckled.

"I have to agree; it's pretty special. But I don't know what we can do."

Abby reached into her dress pocket and brought out a folded brown paper.

"What's that?" Luke asked.

"It's some *tapa* Olani gave me. I . . . uh . . . made another copy of the treasure map . . . just in case we ever needed it." She looked like a cat with the family's pet canary sticking out of its mouth.

Luke threw back his head and gave a big belly-laugh. "I guess your drawings *do* come in handy," he said, shaking his head with wonder. "Abby, was that little scene with you dropping the original map in the ocean all planned?"

She smiled up at him. "I didn't want Jackal to know we had his map. It seemed a good way to settle that issue."

Admiration lit Luke's eyes. "You used to worry about keeping up 'cause of your legs. But I'm getting a mighty strange feeling that you've been setting the pace for all of us."

"Thanks, Luke." Her voice was happy but humble. "I guess you don't have to have the quickest legs in town if you just use the mind God gave you."

Luke sobered then. "That's right. But what are you planning to do with that copy of the map?"

"I thought we might study it a bit this morning, get a good night's sleep, and start out tomorrow on a treasure hunt. My parents really need that gold." Then she added, as if to convince him, "We've got to return Sugar anyway!"

"True. But don't you think we ought to do one more thing before we jump from the frying griddle directly into the fire again?"

"What's that?"

Luke's eyes grazed the waking valley. A single bird trilled a greeting to the early morning. "I thought it might be a good idea to pray about it first."

Surprise filled Abby. "Why, Luke, you're developing into a civilized creature after all! Now if only the Almighty can do something about your snoring. . . ."

As they rose and headed back toward home and the rising scent of coffee and bacon, Luke's indignant voice carried over the quiet land. "*My* snoring! . . . Let me tell you, Abigail, you could rival a thousand frogs who were courting their ladies!"

Abby lifted her chin and sniffed. "Ha! *That* seems a small price to pay for a partner with a map!" Then, gathering her skirts, she raced toward the cabin yelling, "Beat 'cha!"

Luke jumped up to follow, but, as usual, he let her win.

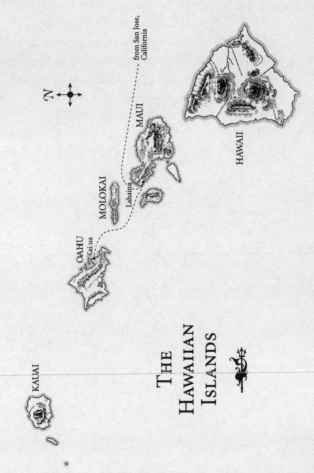

THE
HAWAIIAN ISLANDS

KAUAI

OAHU
Kai ua

MOLOKAI

Lahaina

MAUI

from San Jose,
California

HAWAII

N

Don't miss the next exciting adventure in the South Seas Adventures series:

Will Abby and Luke find gold—or more than they bargained for? And who is that sinister man tailing them?

Hawaiian People, Places, and Words

Follow these two simple rules to say Hawaiian words correctly:

1. Don't end a syllable with a consonant. For example, Honolulu should be pronounced Ho-no-lu-lu, not Hon-o-lu-lu.

2. Say each vowel in a word. The vowels generally are pronounced like this:
   a as in daughter
   e as in prey
   i as in ring
   o as in cold
   oo as in tool

ali'i—Hawaiian chief

aloha—word of welcome or farewell, a type of unconditional love shared

Great Mahele—land division meant to distribute the king's land among commoners and royalty

haole—white foreigner, usually a Caucasian

Hawaii—the largest island of the Hawaiian chain

Kaahumanu—King Kamehameha's favorite wife, who served as queen regent after his death

kahuna—a priest of the Hawaiian religion, or a holy or wise man

kanaka—Hawaiian man or worker (also men)

kiave—tree with sharp thorns which was brought to Hawaii in the 1820s

koa—the largest native tree found in Hawaii's forests

Lanai—small island near Maui and Molokai

Maui—A large island, home of Lahaina, the whaling capital of the Pacific

mauka—toward the mountains

Molokai—one of the three islands that form a natural triangle (with Maui and Lanai)

nani-hair—pretty hair

nui—big

Oahu—A large island in the chain, where Honolulu is located

poi—a Hawaiian staple made from the taro plant

pu-pus—snack foods or hors d'oeuvres

tapa—cloth made from the bark of the paper mulberry tree

wahine—woman or female (also women)

Nautical Words

barkentine—a sailing ship with from three to five masts

berth—bed in a cabin

bow—front of ship

bulkhead—raised portion on deck

duck cloth—a heavy fabric for work clothes

gunwale—the upper edge of a boat

hardtack—dry hard biscuits that travel well on ship

hatchway—a passageway leading from deck to belowdecks

jollyboat—skiff or rowboat used to take sailors from ship to shore

mast—wooden beam which holds up the sails

port—to the left

schooner—a sailing vessel with at least two masts

starboard—to the right, or right side

stern—back of ship

About the Author

Pamela Walls, a freelance writer, fell in love with the Hawaiian people, animals, and islands when she landed a job as a sailor on a sixty-eight-foot sailing ship. "The first time I saw dolphins at the bow, I almost dove overboard," she says. "And the humpback whales were just as curious about me as I was about them."

Inspired, she returned to college and earned a degree in biology and science writing. After years of writing for newspapers and magazines, Pamela began drawing on her adventures in Hawaii to start the Abby series.

"I've looked in the eye of a wild fifty-foot whale, been chased by a two thousand-pound elephant seal, sailed through storms, swum with a dolphin, and leapt off a waterfall (don't try that)! But nothing comes close to the thrill I feel when the Creator of the universe shares His heart with me."

Writing spiritual and realistic stories is her goal, which is why Abby doesn't have a perfect life or body. "Everyone struggles with something," Pamela says, "whether it's physical, emotional, or mental. I happen to have inherited the same leg weakness that Abby has."

That weakness was not discovered and named by doctors until 1886, when three researchers identified it at the same time. Today it's named after those researchers and is known as CMT (Charcot-Marie-Tooth).

CMT affects 150,000 Americans and is found in every people group around the world. Slowly, over a lifetime, CMT patients lose strength in their hands and arms, as well as their feet and legs. Most young people with CMT can walk but have a hard time running and jumping. Many are fitted with leg braces.

Although it was discovered over a hundred years ago, CMT has remained a mystery to the public and, often, the medical community.

"All of my life I've fallen down, twisted my ankle, and generally been a klutz! You should have seen me trying to run relays in P.E.," Pamela says, "because we didn't discover I had CMT until I was an adult."

"But just like Abby, I'm trusting God to help me overcome my limitations. And He's never let me down. Here's the special verse He gave me:

> *His [God's] pleasure is not in the strength of the horse, nor his delight in the legs of a man; the Lord delights in those who fear him, who put their hope in his unfailing love.*
> Psalm 147: 10-11

"Remember, nothing is impossible with God. Whatever *your* challenges are, He will help you when you surrender the situation—and especially your heart—to Him. (See Psalm 116:1-6.)

"I'd love to hear from you! You can write me at: P.O. Box 2492, Hollister, CA 95024-2492."

If you'd like to learn more about CMT, you can contact the CMT Association at 1-800-606-CMTA or CMTAssoc@aol.com.